D0952179

WITCHES AT WAR

The White Wand

MARTIN HOWARD

ILLUSTRATIONS BY COLIN STIMPSON

WITCHES AT WAR II: The White Wand

Text by Martin Howard
Illustrations by Colin Stimpson

First published in 2010 by
Pavilion Children's Books
10 Southcombe Street
London
W14 0RA

An imprint of Anova Books Company Ltd

ISBN 9781843651345

A CIP catalogue record for this book is available
from the British Library.

10 9 8 7 6 5 4 3 2 1

Printed and bound by 1010 Printing International Ltd, China

This book can be ordered direct from the publisher at the website:
www.anovabooks.com
or try your local bookshop.

WITCHES AT WAR

The White Wand

MARTIN HOWARD

ILLUSTRATIONS BY COLIN STIMPSON

PAVILION
CHILDREN'S

Contents

Prologue

Click clack, clickety clack. The sound filled the dark throne room of the Most Superior High and Wicked Witch. *Click clack, clickety clack.* It was accompanied by gloomy sighs and the whispers of a chill draft that crept under doors and through cracks in the cold, stone walls. Violent bursts of hail and snow rattled against tall, arched windows, but still the clicking went on… *click clack, clickety clack.* On the other side of the cracked glass, a gale wailed through the mountains, kicking down trees here, blowing a roof off there, and shaking the thick grey walls of the Bleak Fortress. Tiles were torn from turrets with loud cracks and whirled away on blasts of wind.

In the needle-sharp peaks of Transylvania, winter doesn't arrive with a cheerful jingle of sleigh bells and a quiet puff of fluffy snow. No, Transylvanian winters arrive with a scream and explode like an angry cannon. In Transylvania, winter makes people chew through their bedclothes in terror.

Click clack, clickety clack… Click. The Most Superior High and Wicked Witch, Cakula von Drakula,

stopped knitting and the sound of her knitting needles died away. She sighed, shivered, held up her work and patted her enormous hair-do – which, as usual, had been styled to look like someone had fitted a big, grey bum to her head. Then she nodded slightly and began humming the old vampire song 'I Vanna Suck Your Blud Yeah Yeah Yeah.' She was pleased with what she had been making. Her new woolly cape was black and worked through with a design of great hairy beasts. With a nice pair of mittens, a scarf and some ear muffs, it would help keep her nice and cosy. The Bleak Fortress was colder than a zombie's heart, and at 756-years-old Cakula was beginning to feel the chill in her bones.

With a start, Cakula von Drakula dropped the almost-finished cape into her lap and checked the big, old-fashioned watch fastened to a chain round her neck. She had been so caught up with the knitting that she had almost forgotten that Great Events were about to unfold. She had seen the shape of things yet to come, peeked through the net curtains of time and had a quick glance at impending doom and today was definitely the day for Great Events. Cakula shook the watch. In fact, Great Events were running a bit late…

The great doors of the Bleak Fortress's throne room

slammed open in a glittering burst of magic. Wind screamed into the hall, bringing with it snow, ice, dead leaves and a bewildered chicken that had got caught up in the storm.

Really, thought Cakula to herself, *the draft in here is terrible*. She looked up and saw the figure standing in the doorway. A woman. She was tall, proud and slender, with a shining mane of black hair whipping around her face.

"Goot eeffening Deadly Nightshade," said Cakula. "I haff been hexpecting you." And then, because she *was* a vampire and the weather was perfect for it, she added, "Mwah ha ha HA HAA!"

Diabolica – or 'Deadly' – Nightshade walked across the floor slowly, her stupidly high heels clicking on the bare stone. Only a power-crazed evil sorceress out to take over the world would wear heels like that, and, in fact, Deadly Nightshade was a power-crazed evil sorceress out to take over the world. So that was alright.

Ignoring the traditional vampire laughter, Diabolica came to stand at the foot of the throne. "I've come to take what's mine," she said quietly. "Give me the wand."

"Ze vand? Vut vand?" Cakula gave her a toothy grin. There was a red glow in her eyes like a fire at the end of a long, dark tunnel. Her fingernails drummed on one arm of the throne like jags of broken glass. She looked *all* vampire.

"The Black Wand of Ohh Please Don't Turn Me Into Aaaaargh… Ribbett, of course." Diabolica held out her hand, palm up.

"You know vat? I haffn't seen zat old sing arount for aaages. I vonder vere it got to…"

"One last chance. Give it to me or I'll be forced take it from you." A frown flittered across Diabolica's beautiful face.

"Oh yeah?" jeered Cakula. "You and vitch army?"

Diabolica's frown disappeared. She smiled brightly, stared into Cakula's fiery eyes, and raised her hand. "I'm glad you asked that question. I really am," she giggled. "As a matter of fact, *this* army."

She clicked her fingers. Instantly, a huge Invisibility spell popped and fell away. Behind her stood twenty witches. Every one of them had a dazed, faraway look in her eyes and every one had a wand pointed at The Most Superior High and Wicked Witch.

Cakula was fast. Your average vampire makes a striking snake look like a poorly old lady with heavy shopping. And the Most Superior High and Wicked

Witch was no average vampire. She'd also learned enough about magic in her 756 years that she could turn your head inside out before you had a chance to say "ewww." All in all, Cakula von Drakula was an awesomely, jaw-droppingly powerful vampire-witch. But even she wasn't quick enough to battle twenty witches, all of whom had their wands at the ready and a spell on their lips.

She had just started to raise her knitting when the spell hit. Flashing ropes of purple evil poured from twenty wands and wrapped around her, curling and tightening. The Most Superior High and Wicked Witch was locked in a twisting, sparkling net of pure magic so strong she could neither move or speak. She could glare though, and continued to do so.

Diabolica took another step forward on those ridiculous heels. "Now isn't that interesting," she sniggered. "You tried to defend yourself with some knitting. I wonder why?" Reaching out, she took the knitted cape from Cakula's hand.

There was a faint sparkle from inside the folds of black wool. "Oh no," Diabolica sighed. "You *haven't* been using it as a knitting needle, have you? Oh, you *have*... How vulgar."

Diabolica grasped one of the needles, and pulled it out of the wool, which she let drop to the floor. "Well, well, well, what have we here?" she purred, turning back to Cakula. "If it isn't the Black Wand of Ooh Please Don't Turn Me Into Aaaaarghhh…" she stopped. "Do you know Cakula, I've forgotten the last bit. How does it go again?"

Deadly Nightshade waved the wand. The magical net disappeared and Cakula was surrounded by a swirl of black light. As it ebbed away, a small creature appeared in the shadows.

"Ribbett," croaked The Most Superior High and Wicked Witch.

1 It's All Soooo Unfair!

A young girl sat with her chin in her hands at the kitchen table of a twisty old cottage in the darkest depths of Pigsnout Wood. She was dressed in black jeans and a black jumper and her slightly greasy black hair had fallen, unnoticed, in a cup of tea. A black beetle, named Ringo, was doing star jumps on the brim of her black, patched, and bent pointy hat. Where other witches kept cats or ravens or rats as familiars, this girl had a beetle. A beetle who liked to keep fit.

The girl was frowning and having an argument with a book. Lots of people argue with books. Usually crusty old professors and annoying know-it-alls who say things like, "Of course, Pilkington's *History of Trouser Rotation in the Sixteenth Century* is absolute balderdash and hogwash." This is a bit unfair, because most books can't argue back. But the book the girl was reading, which was called *Think Yourself Witch: 101 Steps Towards Becoming a Crone*, was haunted by the ghost of its author, an ex-witch called Lilith Dwale. Lilith may have been as dead as a spoon, but she wasn't the type of witch who'd let a piffling little thing like not being alive stop

1

her from dropping in for an argument with her granddaughter now and again.

Gritting her teeth and glaring at the book, Lilith's granddaughter asked for the three hundred and sixty-eighth time, "So, if you're my grandmother, who's my mother?"

On the yellow page, scratchy writing wriggled and changed, as if by magic – which, of course, it was. The girl read:

Peeky pokey nosey parker aren't you? I've told you three hundred and sixty seven times already Sam, I can't tell you that. And by the way, your hair's in the tea.

"But that's not fair," Sam hissed, then pulled her hair out of the mug and sucked on it.

Life isn't fair all the time dearest, but let me tell you this instead. And it's important. The first and highest and most serious of witching laws says that witches aren't allowed to have children. There are horrible punishments for anyone that does. But for thousands of years…

"Tut," tutted Sam, spitting out hair. "The last thing

I need is a history lesson, thank *you*."

Above Sam's head the cobwebbed wooden ceiling sagged suddenly. There was a clonk and a shuffling noise and the muffled sound of someone complaining about snails nesting in her hair while she was sleeping. Sam slammed the book shut with another "tut." Esmelia was getting up, and Sam definitely didn't want the old witch knowing about her little talks with Lilith Dwale. Pushing the book aside, she pulled a crumpled letter from her pocket and pretended to be reading that instead.

A door slammed, making the whole cottage shake. Spiders ran to hide in cracks in the walls and one of the windows fell out. Sam rolled her eyes. It sounded like Esmelia was in a one of her moods again.

There was a footstep on the stairs, then a "Mioooowwww" and an "Aaaaarrrrrggghh" as Esmelia Sniff tripped over her cat, Tiddles. With a series of impressively loud bumps, the skinny old witch bounced down the stairs head first, then elbow first, then feet first, then bum first, and came to a stop in a smelly heap of rags at the bottom. Something small and hairy rolled out of the heap and across the floor. A bony, not-very-clean hand reached out and grabbed it. "Drat, drat, DRAT!" screeched Esmelia. "That's me favourite wart. Knocked clean off. I've had that wart for years. It was a part of me, that wart."

A head appeared from out of the heap, and scowled at Sam. A head that looked like someone had stuck a straw in it and sucked. Sam scowled back, which was just asking for trouble. Esmelia was always a teeny bit touchy just after she'd got up. On a good day she was likely to pull the ears off anyone who even breathed in her direction, and she *never* had good days, especially since the Most Superior High and Wicked Witch competition.

Esmelia spotted the letter that Sam was holding. "I told you to stick that on the fire," she sneered as she creaked to her feet. "You ain't goin'. You're *my* apprentice and you'll stay here and do what I tells you. And today I'm telling you to go and dig a hole in the woods then bury yourself up to the neck."

"But *why?*"

Esmelia loomed over her and began counting on her fingers. "First, because it'll make it much easier for me to jump up and down on your head. Second, because you're my apprentice and you does what I tells you, and third… third is the same as number two: 'cos I told you."

Sam's scowl made even deeper lines on her

otherwise pretty forehead and she folded her arms. On the brim of her hat Ringo did the same, though you would have needed a magnifying glass to see his tiny scowl. "I *meant*, why can't I go away," she said sulkily. "Just for a little while. You can't keep me here *all* the time."

A nasty look crossed Esmelia's face, though it was difficult to tell as it was almost exactly the same nasty look as the nasty look that had been there already. "Witchin' law number 2,346, section 3, clause b," she spat. "Once apprenticed to a witch, the apprentice may not leave that witch for any reason whatso-blinkin'-ever, unless either given permission or the apprenticeship is ended by the Most Superior High and Wicked Witch. Furthermore, the apprentice must obey the witch at all times, including when the little cretin is told to go and dig a dirty great hole in the woods and bury herself. Failure to obey will result in the immediate loss of the apprentice's witch license."

Sam stood up and stamped a foot on the floor. Esmelia had discovered this witching law a few weeks ago and had used it about twenty times a day since. On the brim of her hat, Ringo shook a very small fist at the old witch. "But I saved your life," Sam shouted. "You'd be dead now if it weren't for me. Don't you think you should be just a little bit *grateful?*"

Esmelia Sniff bought her face to within an inch of Sam's. "Grateful?" she jeered. "I could've bin Most Superior High and Wicked Witch if it weren't for you and yer peskilential meddling, so you can stick *grateful* in yer ear and wiggle it around." She pushed her face even closer to Sam's until their noses were squashed together and continued in an evil whisper, "And you can tell that little bug of yours if he shakes his fist at me again, I'll squash him like a… like a…" Esmelia struggled for words for a moment then finished, "like a bug," which was a bit lame.

Sam's face twisted in anger. "No," she shouted. "If I hadn't stopped her, Diabolica would have killed you."

"That's what you thinks, but for your information I ain't all that easy to kill. I got a few tricks up me vest."

"Huh, *tricks*," sneered a furious Sam. "That's *all* you've got. Tricks and swearing and meanness. You're so bad at magic Diabolica would have splashed you all over the walls."

"Bah, *magic*," spat Esmelia. "Your type thinks bein' a witch is all sparkles and spangles and hokey pokey. But all that glittery rubbish won't stop a finger in the dark.

Magic ain't no use when someone's poked you in the eye and is swirlin' your eyeball about."

The two witches glared at each other in icy silence.

"Well," Sam said eventually, as calmly as she could manage. "If I'm such a bad apprentice, why don't you just let me go?"

Esmelia's finger jabbed Sam's chest. "Oh yes, you'd *like* that wouldn't you? you little maggot!"

"Yes! Yes I *would* like it," shouted Sam, stamping a foot again. "In fact, I'd *love* it. It would be just fine with me if I never saw your ugly old face again, *especially* when it's eating soup."

"And I'd be happy if I never had to see you sulkin' and mopin' around the place like a sick toad again."

"You're a disgusting, mean and vicious old bag."

"Yes dearie, I knows," replied Esmelia leaning back. "I'm a wicked witch, see? The clue's in the name: *wicked* witch."

Sam turned and stamped towards the door. Esmelia shouted after her, "The spade's in the shed. Proper digging mind, you ain't to use magic. Workin' up a sweat'll teach you a valuable lesson... about sweat or something."

Slamming the door behind her, and with Ringo

gripping the brim of her wonky black hat, Sam ran into the trees. They had lost the last of their leaves and were prodding the cottage's straw roof with bare branches as if testing to see if it was worth eating. Running is never a good idea in Pigsnout Wood though, and the young witch soon tripped over a gnarly old root. She sat on a mossy log, picked thorns out of her legs and brambles from her hair. Once the blood had almost stopped and something with far too many legs had been snorted out of her nose, Sam put her head in her hands and groaned. All her life she'd wanted to be a witch, but now she *was* a witch she was stuck with Esmelia. It was all soooo unfair.

The conversation Sam had been having with her grandmother was completely forgotten. Which was a shame, because Lilith *had* been about to tell her something very important.

2 Smelly Black Clothes, Some Hardly Washed

On most days there was nothing Esmelia liked more than being nasty to her apprentice. It gave her a warm glow in her stomach and a feeling that the day hadn't been wasted. But today, even watching Sam slamming the door in a huff hadn't cheered her up. "I *should've* bin Most Superior High and Wicked Witch," Esmelia muttered to herself as she plonked her skinny backside into a rocking chair by the fire. Clutching the arms she began to rock furiously. "It should be *me* livin' in style at the Bleak Fortress, orderin' everyone around, eatin' pickled bees and wavin' and bein' important."

It had been two months since the Most Superior High and Wicked Witch trials. Two months since Esmelia had been forced to help Sam defeat Diabolica Nightshade and give up her own dreams of winning. After two months most people would have calmed down and sighed and said something like "Oh well, some you win, some you lose," or "It's the taking part that counts", but Esmelia was not that kind of person. She was more the sort that sulked and moaned and took out her annoyance on other people until she was as easy to live with as a wet paper bag full of scorpions.

What she needed, Esmelia decided, was something to brighten her day. Something that would bring a little sunshine into her life and help her enjoy being horrid again. She opened that morning's copy of *The Cackler*, hoping there was a funeral she might invite herself to. A good funeral was always a hoot. She would prefer if it was Cakula von Drakula's funeral, but anything would do at a pinch.

On page after page of the newspaper there was news from the witching world: Diabolica Nightshade still hadn't been caught, some witches had gone missing in Mysterious Circumstances, and two witches had eaten a circus performer. The headline read "CLOWN TASTES FUNNY!" Esmelia groaned and flicked through the pages. There wasn't a single funeral. But a small advert near the bottom of page sixteen caught her eye, and the old witch sat up in her chair. This was more like it. The advert read:

JUMBLE SALE TODAY!!!!
Bargains Galore on Smelly Black Clothes!!!

*All day today in West Wittering Village Hall
we're offering filthy old rags, shoes that don't
match, and dresses what people have probably
died in, judging by the smell. Join your fellow
witches at the tea and cake stand or enjoy a
tug-o-war and a fist-fight over a sock we found
down a drain. Starts at three forty-seven
PM o'clock sharp. First come, first served!!!!*

A jumble sale was even better than a funeral. Esmelia was almost drooling at the thought of black shawls crawling with moths and shapeless old dresses that no one had ever washed. Ever. Jumble sales, in Esmelia's opinion, were what being a witch was all about. She checked the old grandmother clock standing by the wall. It was 3.13. If she hurried she'd be just in time to elbow her way to the front of the queue before the doors opened.

Outside, Sam decided that feeling sorry for herself wasn't helping much. She uncrumpled her letter. It was from her friend Helza Poppin, who had once been the apprentice of the evil, power-crazed sorceress, Diabolica Nightshade. Thanks to Sam, Helza had been released from her apprenticeship by The Most Superior High and Wicked Witch. Sam clenched her fists and wished again that she had asked Cakula von Drakula to end her own apprenticeship with Esmelia. At the time Sam had been feeling sorry for the old bag, and had hoped that she and Esmelia would grow to like each other a bit more. I must have been mad, Sam decided. Over the weeks, she and Esmelia had rowed, argued, quarrelled, bickered and squabbled until the atmosphere in Esmelia's dirty old cottage had started to stink like a box of armpits. Oh well, Sam thought, it was too late now. She stared at the letter in her hands. It read:

Hey Bud

How are you? I'm like totally cool and have a job at a magic store over here in America. The owner is Wisteria Wickham and she's a Wiccan, which is like a witch only she likes to run around the forest with no clothes on. Gross. Apart from that, she's alright and says that you're welcome to visit! It would be awesome if you could come over for a while, plus you could get away from Skanky Sniff. She doesn't like you much anyway, so she should be happy to let

you go.
     Love n' kisses BFF
     Helza Poppin XXX

"What Helza forgets, Ringo," Sam growled. "Is that Esmelia's a miserable old ratbag who hates seeing anyone else happy. She'll keep me here forever if she thinks there's even a tiny chance I might go and enjoy myself."

At that moment, the door of the cottage slammed open and a familiar voice screeched, "Oi you! Thingammyjig whatever-yer-name-is apprentice. I'm off to a jumble sale. I'll be back late so when you've buried yerself, wait there 'til I gets back."

There was a snapping of branches as Esmelia's broom took to the skies. Sam glared after it. The old witch turned and made a rude gesture at her before disappearing into grey clouds. At that moment Sam decided that she had had more than enough of the disgusting old biddy. Although it was completely against all the rules, she *would* go and ask Cakula to release her from her apprenticeship.

Sam glanced at her watch. Even if the Most Superior High and Wicked Witch said "no," she should get back before Esmelia anyway. A jumble sale would keep the old bag occupied for *hours*. If she didn't get back in time she would be in *real* trouble though. There would be cackling, sneering and poking, and if Esmelia reported her to the Witches' Licensing Bureau (and she would, just to be mean) Sam would have her license taken away and have to go back to living in the orphanage.

On the other hand, the Most Superior High and Wicked Witch, might say "yes" and then Sam would be *free*.

It was *definitely* worth the risk. Holding up her beetle on a finger, Sam said, "Do you fancy a trip?"

In reply, Ringo took Sam's nose in his front legs and planted a very small kiss on the end of it. Sam giggled. Then she whistled quietly. A broom swept out of the cottage's attic window and stopped in front of her, at just the right height to swing a leg over. Tucking Ringo safely under her jumper and jamming her hat down tightly, Sam settled on the broom's handle and said, "Transylvania, please."

3 Foul Play

Sam's broom was one-of-a-kind. It had been handmade by Lilith Dwale, when she wasn't too dead to do things like make brooms, and was probably the fastest bundle of twigs tied to a stick ever to take to the skies. But even Lilith's amazing broom was having difficulties in the teeth of a Transylvanian winter. Cold seeped through its protective spell and the bullying wind kept trying to push Sam into mountain peaks hidden by whirling sheets of ice and snow.

While Ringo shivered under her vest, puffing on his feet and going "brrrrr" very quietly, Sam gripped the handle and tried to stay on course. Slowly, she flew onwards, keeping half an eye on her watch.

For a few seconds Sam let her mind wander away from trying to stay upright in the storm. If Cakula said "yes," she thought, it would be nice to get home first just to see the look on Esmelia's face when she landed outside the cottage. When she heard that Sam was no longer her apprentice she would go completely *bonkers*…

No, said Sam to herself firmly. It would be *nasty* to enjoy the sight of Esmelia eating her own hat – and possibly her fingers too – in fury. Sam had promised herself she wouldn't be the type of witch who liked seeing other people upset, no matter how much they deserved it.

A fierce gust of wind nearly threw her into an especially jagged rock. Sam's attention snapped back to the broom and she couldn't help a squeal of fear as it dodged sharply, then dodged again as a roof tile came spinning out of the dark clouds straight at her head. For an instant the curtain of snow parted, just long enough for Sam to glimpse the great dark bulk of the Bleak Fortress clinging to a high mountain.

She'd made it.

Two minutes later the young witch shivered on the steps beneath the Great Entrance to the stronghold of the Most Superior High and Wicked Witch. Above her stretched huge doors, thirty foot high, a foot thick and carved with skulls. Both were swinging open in the gale. Ringo poked his head out of Sam's jumper briefly and clicked his pincers. "I was wondering about that too, Ringo," shouted Sam above the roar of wind. "You'd think someone would notice the draft."

"Hello! Anyone home?" Sam shouted as she crossed into the entrance hall, then, just in case, added "Any chance of some hot chocolate?"

The wind tore the words out of her mouth and blew them, echoing, along empty stone corridors. No one replied. Things were obviously not right at the Bleak Fortress and, with witches being involved, things not being right almost certainly meant foul play. Sam cursed quietly under her breath. She'd been hoping for a quick chat with Cakula then home in time to pack up her belongings before Esmelia arrived. Foul play was the last thing she needed, but if it was afoot then it was best to be prepared.

Sam slipped her wand from her back pocket. Ringo ran up to her shoulder and together they prepared an Escape spell, setting it to the place where Sam stood. If peril threatened or danger pounced or terror reared its unattractive head, she would be able to instantly magic herself back to the entrance hall. When the spell had been cast, she leaned her broom against a wall then turned to creep up the vast, winding staircase.

Apart from a bat that chittered past her head and almost got spelled into a small smoking cinder by a jumpy Sam, there was no one to be seen. The Bleak Fortress seemed completely empty. Keeping to the shadows and with her wand held at the ready, Sam tip-

toed down a long corridor peeking around doors now and again. There were torture chambers, dungeons and a grim lavatory with a knitted cosy over the toilet roll, but no sign of Cakula von Drakula.

Finally, Sam peered around another grand door that was hanging open. On the other side was the biggest room she had ever seen. The ceiling rose in complicated stonework, with crooked pillars holding up a roof from which the carved shapes of hideous drooling things stared down. Most young girls would have been knee-knockingly petrified at the very sight of them, but Sam had seen Esmelia eating and the hideous drooling things weren't half as bad. All was dim and – apart from the noise of dead leaves rustling in the icy draft and a chicken squawking in a corner – silent.

"I don't think the Most Superior High and Wicked Witch is at home Ringo," Sam whispered nervously to the beetle on her shoulder.

Ringo bobbed up and down in agreement.

Sam was just about to withdraw her head and make her way back to the entrance hall when something twitched in the corner of her sight. Before a great throne was a small mound of what looked like black wool. And it had *hopped*.

Knowing that even the best of jumble sales wouldn't keep Esmelia busy forever, but too curious to stop herself, Sam looked about quickly then scurried across the stone floor. It was wool, and looked like someone had been knitting a black blanket. And there was something moving in it. Kneeling, Sam gently parted the wool with her fingers. There, trembling from cold, was a frog. It looked up at her. Sam reached out her hands. The frog croaked unhappily and hopped onto her palms.

Sam stood, cradling the poor freezing creature to her jumper and, feeling a little stupid, whispered, "I don't suppose you're a talking frog, are you? Only it would be great if you could tell me where Cakula von Drakula is."

"Ribbett," said the frog.

"Fine, fine. Silly of me to ask I suppose."

Sam stood up to leave, then froze. From the corridor outside came the *click, click, click* of ludicrously high heels.

4 The Ghastly Threat of Befroggination

The clicking came closer quickly. Now Sam could hear a voice. A voice that sounded like melting chocolate and was ever-so horribly familiar. A voice that purred, "For badness sake, would one of you mindless zombie things *please* close the door, and light some torches, it's *terribly* chilly and dingy in here..." A voice that got louder with every clicking footstep. "Now, I think we'll hang the big portrait of me wearing the black spider fur gown there... And perhaps another portrait here. The one where I'm summoning face-eating demons and wearing that simply *gorgeous* red dress would look nice. What do you think Mandy?"

Sam stiffened, the frog still clutched to her chest. *It couldn't be*, she thought. *Not here. Not so soon after she had been defeated.*

But it was.

Diabolica Nightshade stepped through the door.

"You!" gasped Sam.

"You!" gasped Diabolica.

"Or maybe the portrait with the *other* black dress and Mr Popsy on your lap your gorgeously pouting wickedness..." said Mandy Snoutley as she walked into Diabolica's back. Diabolica's henchperson, the ex-reporter from *The Cackler*, was as old and hideous as Sam remembered her, and still dressed like a teenage pop sensation.

Behind Mandy was a crowd of witches. Each was staring with her mouth hanging open and a blank look in her eyes as if she had spent an entire day in maths class. Sam stared back in stunned surprise. It gave Diabolica time to pull a slim length of sparkling black from her sleeve: The Black Wand of Ohh Please Don't Turn Me Into Aaaarghh... Ribbett.

Sam glanced from the wand to the frog she held in her hands. "Oh no," she whispered. "You didn't?"

"Oh yes, I did," smiled Diabolica tapping her lips with the wand.

"Oh no, you didn't."

"Oh yes, I *did*," Diabolica insisted.

"Oh no..."

"Please child," interrupted Diabolica. "Just take my word for it, I *did* turn the vampire into a frog. And it was probably for the best. I mean, that hair-do. Sooo five hundred years ago. Vampires should have *style*, don't you think?"

Mandy Snoutley's face peered out from behind Diabolica. "Go on. Befrogginate the plot-foiling little twerp," she hissed.

"Hush Mandy. I'm enjoying the moment and toying with the victim." Diabolica turned back to Sam. "Now where was I? Oh yes... so now *I'm* going to be Most Superior High and Wicked Witch, you see? Which is what was *supposed* to have happened two months ago. And do you know what I *promised* myself? What I've been looking forward to the most?"

Sam felt like she ought to say something clever, but the only answer to Diabolica's question she could think of was "a nice cup of tea", which wasn't very clever at all. Instead, knowing that it would make her look like an idiot, Sam shook her head.

"I promised myself that once I'd dealt with the badly-dressed vampire then it would be *your* turn... You and that dreadful Sniff baggage," Diabolica sneered. "And that ex-apprentice of mine, Igor or Helza or whatever she calls herself now."

She lifted The Black Wand of Ohh Please Don't Turn Me Into Aaaarghh... Ribbett. "Before I befrogginate you... as Mandy puts it... can I just say thank you *so* much for coming, you saved me a long journey in the cold and wet. Now, talking of cold and wet..."

A furious bolt of magic hurtled towards Sam. Luckily, at that moment she stopped shaking her head and found exactly the right thing to say.

"Escape!"

A spiral of white light swept around Sam so quickly it was over almost before it had begun. The throne room disappeared and the magic pouring from The Black Wand of Ohh Please Don't Turn Me Into Aaaarghh... Ribbett cascaded through the space where she had been and into a corner where an already upset chicken suddenly found its day had got even worse. "Ribbett," it clucked sadly to itself.

Back in the entrance hall, Sam heard a shriek of rage from above. "After her! Everyone! She can't have gone far with that spell. To your brooms. *NOW*!" screamed Diabolica.

For a second, Sam stared at the vampire-witch-frog in her hands, realising that she had a problem. Sam's jeans had small pockets and she had no bag. Oh well, she thought, there was nothing else for it. Gritting her teeth, she stuffed the clammy amphibian up her jumper and tried not to notice it squirming as she reached for her broomstick.

With a blast of wind in her face, the young witch raced out the gigantic doors and fled into the storm. Behind her, windows smashed and glass scattered as a small army of witches took to the sky in pursuit. Wands flashed in the gloom and the air around Sam burned and sizzled with jets of colour as the broom dodged spell after spell.

"You can't escape," screeched Diabolica. "You're *mine*!"

"Oh no I'm not!" shouted Sam over her shoulder, as she leaned over her broom and urged it higher and faster.

"Oh *yes* you are!"

"Oh no I'm… oh forget it."

Sam sped into the evening sky. This time the storm was behind her and it flung the broom out of the mountains at a speed no other broomstick could have hoped to match. Even so, she knew Diabolica wouldn't be far behind. And with her army of witches and The Black Wand of Ohh Please Don't Turn Me Into

Aaaarghh… Ribbett in her hands, Sam knew there was nothing she could do to stop the power-crazed evil sorceress. She had to get as far away as she could as quickly as possible. And she had to warn Helza.

Sam turned the broom towards the Atlantic Ocean and America. Then another thought struck her: *But what about Esmelia?*

What about *the old ratbag?* replied another part of her brain.

For a few seconds Sam's mind argued amongst itself. Then, with a groan, she pulled the broomstick's handle round.

5 Eat the Witch

"Ooooo Tiddles, would you just look at that. Some steaming great ninny's thrown away a perfectly good pair of knickers just because the elastic's gone and there's a couple of holes and a slug or two."

Tiddles took a sniff at the long bloomers Esmelia was holding up and keeled over onto the floor, where he lay with his legs in the air. "There's plenty of wear left in *them*," Esmelia continued. "And look at this lovely vest, it's got the lot: dried sweat, yellow stains, even old bits of egg stuck all over the front. And me feeling a bit peckish too…"

Esmelia spied movement out of the corner of her eye. She stopped rummaging through her Jumble Sale Party Fun Bag and grabbed the poker. With a muttered, "Oh no you doesn't," she thwhacked a sock that was crawling across the kitchen table, then thwhacked it again, and again, until it had stopped twitching. Once she was sure it wasn't going to attack her, she picked it up and held it to her nose.

"Aaaaah," she crooned blissfully. "I ain't smelled nothin' like that since that badger died behind the sink.

It was a stroke of luck findin' a sock like that."

Tiddles had stopped moving and gone stiff, but Esmelia hadn't noticed. "*And* it was only fifty-eight pee for the lot," she cackled. "Though, of course I pinched me money back when no one was lookin'." She jingled her purse. "Plus another twenty-six pounds and thirty-two pence."

The jumble sale had been everything Esmelia had hoped it would be. She'd had drunk sixteen cups of tea, eaten enough gingerbread to build a small bungalow and had a fight over a china kitten with only two legs missing. Esmelia sighed happily at the memory. The other witch had eventually been led away with a black eye, two broken fingers, and a china kitten wedged up her nose. *Good times*, thought Esmelia. In fact, she was in such a cheerful mood she could hardly wait to start being mean to her apprentice. She cocked her head to one side, listening. It was very quiet in the cottage. For a moment she wondered where the nasty little sniveller was lurking, then remembered she had told Sam to go and bury herself in the woods.

"Well, Tiddles," Esmelia said, ignoring the fact that her cat was now thrashing about and foaming at the mouth. "I'll just have a quick cup of tea then go and smear some jam on the whippersnapper's head, shall I? Nothing quite like jam for attracting them stinging ants."

Esmelia set the old, black kettle on the stove to boil, and spread her jumble out over the table. Near the bottom of the sack was a false beard that might once have turned someone into a jolly Father Christmas, but now looked like it had been made entirely from belly button fluff. It was grey and streaked with stains and dirt but as soon as she'd seen it the beard had given Esmelia a tremendous idea.

She fitted the hooked wires over her ears and went to inspect herself in the cracked mirror. "Oooo Tiddles, don't I look dashing? Just like *him*."

She paused for a moment and then murmured, by way of practice, "Hello little boy. Would you like to sit on Esmelia's... sorry... *Santy's* knee? And what's Santy Claws got in his sack for you, eh? Ooooo look at that, it's a packet of stuffing and a bonk on the head."

Esmelia's shoulders heaved with laughter. *Oh yes*, she thought, *a beard like that might come in very useful*. She put her hand up and stroked it thoughtfully. And it really did suit her. Maybe she should keep it on for a while, just to get used to it of course...

THE WHITE WAND

The door crashed open, making Esmelia squeal. She whirled round furiously and grabbed a deadly sock to throw at whoever was disturbing her beard fitting.

"Oh, it's *you*," she grumped, seeing Sam standing in the doorway. The girl was wheezing and wild-eyed and had her mouth hanging open like a loony, Esmelia noted. She was also quite pleased to see Sam had crazy hair and appeared to have been dragged through a hedge backwards, then forwards, backwards again and then rolled around a bit just to make sure. She was carrying a frog too. *Perhaps there is some hope for the little twonk after all*, the old witch thought. Still, an order was an order. "I thought I told you to go and bury yourself," Esmelia screeched. "Why ain't you up to your neck in mud?"

"Esmelia, there's no time to explain... *why* are you wearing a false beard... no there's no time for that either. Diabolica's on her way and she's got The Black Wand of Ohh Please Don't Turn Me Into Aaaarghh... Ribbett. We have to get out of here. Now!"

"I mean, I was just coming to smear jam on your head and now you've gone and ruined my day. *Again*." Esmelia sulked, threatening Sam with the sock. "And look what you've done to Tiddles, banging around the place like that. You've given the poor little mite a heart attack."

"Esmelia!" Sam shouted. "Listen to me. Diabolica's coming *here*. *Now*. Look!" She held Cakula von Drakula under Esmelia's nose.

The old witch seemed to calm down a little. She sniffed the frog and snorted, "Young people today! Always thinking about food, food, food. Well I *was* going to have some egg, but seeing as how you've gone to the trouble I suppose I could manage a leg or two…"

"You can't *eat* it! It's Cakula von Drakula, you great warty idiot," Sam shrieked.

Esmelia was impressed, despite herself. The girl's shriek was coming along nicely. A shriek like that was a shriek a witch could be proud of. And she was gibbering complete nonsense, too, which was promising. Gibbering nonsense was another important skill for a witch.

"Cakula von Drakula!" Sam shrieked again, almost pushing the frog up Esmelia's nose. The old witch started to drool a little bit. "Diabolica's turned Cakula into a frog and now she's coming to do the same to us!" screeched Sam. Her shoulders sagged in relief as understanding finally flickered in Esmelia's eyes.

"Sooooo," the old witch said slowly. "You're telling me… that this here plump and delicious frog what you're holding, is none other than Cakula von Drakula, the Most Superior High and Wicked Witch… Is that what you're telling me?"

"Yes!" screamed Sam, "Yes, yes, yes, yes, YES!"

Esmelia pouted. "Pah, I don't see why *that* should stop us eatin' it."

From outside came the sound of branches breaking as Diabolica Nightshade, Mandy Snoutley and twenty zombie witches dropped out of the evening sky.

"Aaaarrgh," gibbered Sam. "She's here, she's *here*. We're going to be befrogginated!"

Esmelia crossed her arms. *Excellent*, she thought; *the little maggot's gibberish was coming along nicely.*

6 Inside A Hag 3000

"You there… Yes you, *you* shuffling mindless thing. Take the other shuffling mindless things and search the place," ordered Diabolica Nightshade as she strolled into Esmelia's cottage with her small shuffling army shuffling behind her. "They must still be here somewhere, look the kettle's just started boiling."

Diabolica stood in the middle of Esmelia's grim kitchen as her glassy-eyed followers shuffled up the stairs and began opening wardrobes and prodding about under beds and in chests with fingers like sticks of limp celery, "Oh would you look at this, Mandy?" Diabolica continued grouchily while bending over. "These shoes are *ruined*. Why on earth would any *real* witch choose to live like a rat in such a hovel?"

"Esmelia's one of the old sort, your nibbliness. They like living in filth and muck. It's traditional. Same with the warts and the big noses."

"It'll all be different when I'm ruling the world Mandy. The old sort who live like rats will be *exterminated* like rats." Diabolica had started prowling around the kitchen. "Come out come out wherever you are," she giggled and sniffed the air. "I can *smell* yo... aaaarrrgh, Mandy what is that *revolting* stink?"

"I think it's coming from those old rags," Mandy replied, pointing at Esmelia's jumble.

Diabolica had already lost interest. "Now where would I be hiding if I were an irritating nosey parker..." she murmured. "Of course, I wouldn't be *hiding* anywhere. I'd have cast an Invisibility spell." She smiled, whipped The Black Wand of Ohh Please Don't Turn Me Into Aaaarghh... Ribbett around her head, and shouted, "*Coming*, ready or not!"

A black shadow spread from the wand and filled the cottage. Any other magic it touched immediately crumbled away, invisibility spells included...

... The black shadow lifted.

"Oh," said Diabolica Nightshade, then "Drat." Everything in the cottage was exactly as before (except under Esmelia's bed where a box containing dozens of copies of *Wizard Hunks Monthly* magazine had magically appeared). Sam and Esmelia were still nowhere to be seen.

As Diabolica had been turning the door handle to the cottage, Sam had bundled Esmelia into the oven then squeezed in after. Luckily, Esmelia had a Hansel and Gretel Industries HaG 3000 SuperStove, which was, as the brochure said, "Big Enough to Fit Even the Gangliest Teenager," or – as it turned out – just big enough to fit two witches, a cat, a large frog, and a beetle, though not in comfort.

"Gahh, get yer knee out of me ear," whispered Esmelia fiercely.

"I can't move or I'll squash Cakula," hissed Sam.

"It's disgustin' this oven, I thought I told you to clean it out last week."

"I *did* clean it out, but that was before your Stinging Nettle Surprise exploded in here."

"That *was* a surprise though, weren't it?"

There was a huuuurggh huuuurggh huuuurggh noise in the dark, and a pause. "Oh, good grief," muttered Sam. "Tiddles has been sick in my hair."

"That's nice," murmured Esmelia. "A bit of cat sick adds volume and makes difficult hair easier to manage. I bin using it for years." She paused for a second, then continued, "I don't mind bein' pushed in the oven. It's all part of bein' a witch bein' pushed in the oven and it's good to keep in practice. But just so's you know for next time, you're not s'posed to get in as well."

"Shush," shushed Sam. She'll hear us."

"Who'll hear us?" Esmelia put her bony finger to the glass front of the oven. There was a tiny squeaking sound as she made a small circle in the grime. Putting one eye to the hole, she grumped, "What's *she* doin' in *my* cottage?"

"I was trying to tell you, but you never listen to me."

"Strollin' in as bold as monkeys with a... Oooo is that The Black Wand of Ohh Please Don't Turn Me Into Aaaarghh... Ribbett she's got? Has she pinched it?"

Sam sighed. "You *never* listen to me," she repeated. "And, by the way, I just saved your life *again*."

Meanwhile, Mandy Snoutley had been inching her way towards the pile of jumble on the kitchen table. She was *sure* there would be nothing in it at all to suit her, but all the same it *was* a big pile of smelly clothes and a little rummage wouldn't do any harm. It had been a long time since she had been to a jumble sale. Perhaps she might even have a little *sniff*...

"Mandy, what *are* you doing?" squealed Diabolica. "Come away before you catch something."

Mandy snatched a sock away from her nose and looked up guiltily. "I was... err... *investigating* your supreme... umm... supremeness," she said, prodding the mound. "Look, I found this old book."

"Hmmm, *Think Yourself Witch: 100 Steps Towards Becoming a Crone* by Lilith Dwale," said Diabolica taking it from Mandy's hands. "Never heard of it, but didn't Lilith Dwale gave Sam a recommendation for the Most Superior High and Wicked Witch Trials? There's something going on there, it might be useful. Well done Mandy."

Mandy grinned, and stuffed the sock into her handbag while Diabolica flicked through the pages.

From somewhere came a scrabbling noise. Someone with very very good hearing might have heard a furious muffled voice saying, "She's pinchin' my sock! I nearly paid for that sock. I'll break her blinkin' legs..."

"What was that?" Diabolica said sharply, lifting her head. Inside the oven, Sam slapped her hand over Esmelia's mouth. All was silent again, except for the sound of shuffling on the stairs.

"Mice, probably," said Mandy Snoutley. "Or rats or bats or maybe it was your gormless army of the brain dead marching down the stairs."

Diabolica gave her henchperson a sharp look. Mandy spluttered, and added, "... your smashingness."

"Hmmm," replied Diabolica, then turned to the

last witch as the rest trooped out of the front door. "Well?" she demanded. "Did any of you find anything?"

The witch turned her unblinking gaze on Diabolica and dropped half a set of false teeth into her waiting hand. "Teeeeef," she droned in a voice that sounded like it had echoed around a maggoty grave. "Pretty teeeef."

"Ugh," said Diabolica, dropping them quickly.

"Looks like Sam and Esmelia got away then," said Mandy, brightly.

"Unfortunately, you seem to be right. Curses," spat Diabolica. "But I'll find them, especially that vile Sam girl. She *ruined* the Most Superior High and Wicked Witch Trials and what sort of power-crazed evil sorceress would I be if I didn't get revenge? When I find her, I'll make her wish she'd never been born…"

Diabolica paused for a moment, sucked the end of The Black Wand of Ohh Please Don't Turn Me Into Aaaarghh… Ribbett thoughtfully, then continued, "That gives me an idea. No one had ever heard of Sam until a couple of months ago, but she must have come from somewhere. Mandy, I want you to find out everything you can about that horrid little toad. Where she came from, who her family are, where she's likely to go. Wherever she tries to hide, she'll find me waiting for her."

Mandy's nodding became more excited. "Oh yes, your deadliness. I'm good at stuff like that. Trust Mandy to find out all there is to find out."

"Good Mandy, then Sam and Esmelia will be in our clutches soon, and in the meantime, let's make absolutely sure they're not hiding in here somewhere, shall we?"

"But how are we going to do that your soft, quilted velvetiness?"

Diabolica raised The Black Wand of Ohh Please Don't Turn Me Into Aaaarghh... Ribbett. "Fire," she purred. A stream of flame poured from the tip of the wand. The cottage, which was mostly made from old twigs, straw, and owl droppings, was ablaze in seconds.

With the fire leaping higher and higher around her, Diabolica tucked *Think Yourself Witch* under her arm and turned to her henchperson. "Make sure you find out *everything*," she said with the reflections of flames dancing in her eyes. "Now, let's be off shall we? I have a world to take over. Busy, busy, busy..."

7 Spankbaskets and Toad Bums

The door of Esmelia's oven fell open with a clang. A smoking tangle of witches, frog, cat and beetle tumbled out in a struggling heap that swore and meowed and croaked for a few minutes as everyone tried to sort out whose arms and legs were whose. Eventually, they stood up, faces covered in soot and the black crumbs of petrified Stinging Nettle Surprise.

THE WHITE WAND

For a moment there was silence as the little group stared around them. What had been Esmelia's home for as long as she could remember was a wide patch of cinders, with a few timbers still smouldering and an old cauldron clinking as it cooled down. The cottage had burned like a moth in a flamethrower and taken with it everything that Esmelia and Sam owned. Only the heavy iron and thick glass of the HaG 3000 had saved them from being burned to crispy crispiness.

"Me jumble," screeched Esmelia clutching the sides of her head. "Me precious jumble." Then, "Me house. Me precious cottage."

Sam didn't answer. Her hatred of Diabolica was almost boiling over. Gritting her teeth and clenching her fists, she gaped round at the ruins with

tears of rage in her eyes. Everything had gone: her clothes, her peaceful attic bedroom with its mess of old claptrap, her books and her… *book. Think Yourself Witch* had been stolen. The only way Sam could talk to Lilith Dwale was now in the evil grasp of Diabolica Nightshade. "Oh, grandmother," she whispered.

Esmelia, on the other hand, was not in a whispering mood. Her face had gone a very deep green and her eyes were almost popping out of her head. She was jumping up and down on the ashes of her home, pulling out great clumps of her own hair. In a strangled voice the old witch squealed, "Aaarggghh… spankbaskets and toad bums… drooling bags of dogs doings tied up round the middle… of all the widdle-brained donkey bottom fiddlers…"

It looked like she might actually explode. Sam forced herself to calm down and put a gentle hand on the old witch's arm. "It's alright," she said. "We'll find a way to get even with Diabolica."

"Not her, *you* you steaming mound of goblin poo," screamed the old witch. "It's all your fault."

Sam gasped. "*My* fault? How can it be my fault? *I* didn't burn the cottage down."

Esmelia stopped hopping up and down and

pointed a bony finger of blame at Sam. "It's your meddlin' and pokin' about and stickin' your nose in what caused this. If you hadn't started meddlin' and pokin' about and stickin' your nose in I'd be Most Superior High and Wicked Witch and that Diddlybolica would be hangin' upside down by her toenails in me dungeon with rats nibblin' at her eyebrows."

Sam burst into tears. It had been that kind of a day.

Esmelia was taken aback. She was used to fighting. She *liked* fighting. And this was the point in a fight when slaps were usually exchanged, followed by hair pulling and squealing. Her opponents didn't usually sink to their knees and start weeping. At least, not until Esmelia had poked them in the eye. Sam was taking all the fun out of it and the old witch didn't know what to do. Worse than that, Esmelia was horrified to find that deep down inside, a tiny, miniscule, weeny part of her was almost feeling like maybe, perhaps, she ought to pat the crying girl on the head and say "there, there," or something. It was such a shock, Esmelia felt quite faint.

"Why do witches have to be so *nasty*?" sobbed Sam between her fingers.

Esmelia shrugged her bony shoulders. Sam might as well have asked why fishes had to be so wet. Then she stared at her hand, which – without her even thinking about it – had reached out to pat Sam's head. "Got to be nasty," she mumbled in a panic, "'s'like fish."

Through her sobs Sam wondered what Esmelia was babbling about. She looked up saw a trembling hand reaching out.

"Thank you," sniffed the apprentice. She took Esmelia's hand and pulled herself to her feet, blowing her nose on a sleeve. "So, what are we going to do now? Diabolica will be looking for us everywhere."

Esmelia furiously wiped her hand on her dress and mumbled to herself, "wasn't helpin' you blubberin' little insect."

Sam wasn't listening. She had remembered something. Something important. "Oh no," she cried. "Helza!"

"Bless you."

"It wasn't a sneeze. You remember Helza Poppin, my friend who makes the potions? Diabolica said she would be after her too."

Esmelia's eyes narrowed. "I din't hear her say nothin' of the sort."

Sam blushed and looked down at her feet. "She sort of said it at the Bleak Fortress earlier," she muttered.

"Eh?"

"I went to the Bleak Fortress to see if Cakula would release me from being your apprentice, but I was too late and Diabolica was already there and I…"

"… led her straight to my cottage," finished Esmelia, scowling.

"No. It wasn't like that! I had to choose to warn you or Helza first, and I… well, I chose to warn you." Under her breath she added, "which was really stupid of me."

Esmelia's face turned stony. The urge to reach out and throttle Sam was almost too much to bear. But a part of her brain was jumping up and down and trying to get her attention. *When all this is over, maybe you won't need no cottage*, it was cackling. *Maybe you'll be livin' at the Bleak Fortress after all.*

She looked down at the frog in Sam's hands and tiny wicked glints flickered in her eyes. With Cakula von Drakula out of the way, all that stood between her and being Most Superior High and Wicked Witch was Diabolica Nightshade, and if she couldn't out-witch that primping ninny then her name wasn't Esmelia Sniff. Especially if she had help. Esmelia had to admit that her apprentice had become very good at magic, and the potions girl might be of some use too.

In silence, Esmelia's two teeth gnashed together. Finally, the old witch grumped, "Alright. We'll see about gettin' yer friend, but only 'cos she might be useful. I ain't bein' *nice* or nuthin'."

"Thank you Esmelia," replied Sam. "What are we going to do about Diabolica though."

"What we needs is a plot. A plot what will let me jump up and down on that Dreary Lampshade's face singin' "the broken bone is connected to the broken bone," song. First though we got to find somewhere to hide for the night. And I knows just the place."

Sam nodded and whistled for her broom.

Esmelia also whistled for her broom. A twisted and blackened twig at her feet rose about a foot in the air, spun lazily in circles and puffed into a small cloud of ash.

"You can share mine," said Sam kindly. "Oh, and Esmelia?"

"What now?"

"Why *are* you wearing a false beard?"

Esmelia stroked the bedraggled mess on her chin thoughtfully, then said slowly, "That's Esmelia's little secret dearie, but I think it might come in handy... oh yes, very handy indeed."

8 A Night At The Goblin's Elbow

Esmelia's knuckles rapped sharply on polished wood that glowed under soft candlelight. "Hello," she screeched. Realising that she sounded too much like a witch she tried again in a deeper voice that sounded like a large dog being strangled. "Hello? Hello? Wizards lookin' for a room here."

The landlord of the Goblin's Elbow stood up behind the counter. He was bald apart from two bits of ginger hair that stuck out like wings at either side of his head and was wearing a tie on which was written, "You Don't Have To Be Mad To Work Here... But I Am!..." He was grumbling, "alright, alright, I'm not deaf you..." Then he looked into Esmelia's face and continued... "Uuuurghh."

Lionel Ulcer was a man who had seen some horrible things during a lifetime working at the inn for magical folk – headless horsemen, spooks that haunted your trousers, and his wife's sister among them – but he'd never seen anything like Esmelia. He clutched at the desk in front of him, staring at the filthy, bearded, pointy-hatted witch in front of him. Little wisps of *smoke* were coming off her. Finally, he managed to gabble out, "Yes madam… how may I help you?"

"Sir," growled Esmelia.

"What?" gurgled Lionel Ulcer.

"It's sir, not madam you cheeky beggar. I got a beard, see," hissed the old witch, then continued in her best deep voice, "I am the wizard…" She stopped. She had forgotten to think up a false name to go with her disguise. "Es… no… Jeffrey… *bums*… errr…" Esmelia stuttered. She glanced round the inn looking for inspiration, "umm… Hatstand. Esnojeffreybumser Um Hatstand. Yes, that's me. And this is my apprentice… err…"

"Sam," interrupted Sam quickly. She was wearing jeans and had just stuffed her hair up under her hat as a disguise. Which would have been fine, but as she had a broomstick under her arm and was carrying a black cat and a large frog, her disguise wouldn't have fooled a man wearing sunglasses on a moonless night either.

Landlords of inns for magical folk learn not to ask questions though, especially of witches. Witches, in Lionel's experience, were always a bit batty. *Granted*, he thought, *usually not as batty as this pair, but none of them were quite right in the head.* "Right you are… *gentlemen,*" he said slowly. "Will you be wanting a room with a bath?"

"N…" Esmelia began.

"Yes. Thankyou," finished Sam firmly.

"No," insisted Esmelia. "Baths give you the scurvy, plus there's always the danger of melting."

"A room without a bath for one night'll be twenty-six pounds and thirty-two pence." Then, because he was a man who had met plenty of witches, Lionel Ulcer added, "And you have to pay now."

Esmelia gave a high-pitched squeal of outrage, "*How* much? You theivin' little worm…" She cleared her throat and went on in her strangled-dog voice, "I mean that seems rather expensive, my good man."

"And it's fifty-eight pee for breakfast," said Lionel Ulcer holding out his hand.

After Esmelia's fingers were prised, one by one, from her purse, the two witches had been shown to a comfortable room. When Lionel Ulcer had gone, muttering that them as thought *he* was mad should catch an eyeful of his new guests, Esmelia settled herself by the fire and leaned over a small cauldron. She gave it an experimental stir, a sure sign that a plot was beginning to form.

"So, what's the plan then?" asked Sam, twitching impatiently. "Shall I rescue Helza? Then we'll steal back The Black Wand of Ohh Please Don't Turn Me Into Aaaarghh... Ribbett, turn Cakula back and let her deal with Diabolica? Cakula will be so grateful she'll rebuild your cottage for you, won't you Cakula?"

"Ribbett," said Cakula, from a pillow on the four-poster bed.

Esmelia looked up at her apprentice. Despite her cottage being burned to the ground, she was feeling almost cheerful. Plotting over a bubbling cauldron always did the trick. She *did* have a plan and, as far as Esmelia was concerned, it was a doozy, though it wasn't quite the same the plan that Sam had suggested. *Her* plan involved a lot more eye-poking and ended with Esmelia Sniff being Most Superior High and Wicked Witch. It was a *good* plan. And this time she wouldn't let Sam, Diabolica, or Cakula von Drakula ruin it.

Nevertheless, Esmelia snickered, "Oh yes dearie. That's *exakkerly* what I was thinkin'. That's a *luvverly* plan that is. I'm sure I don't know how you does it, comin' up with brilliant plans like that."

Sam interrupted her. Diabolica was probably on the way to befrogginate Helza and she had to get there first. "I'd better go and find Helza then," she said quickly.

"Well, wrap up warm dearie it's a long way to America by broom."

Sam shook her head. "Broom will take too long and Diabolica has a head start." She lifted her wand. "I'm going to use the Gammer Widdle's Fantastical Portal spell and turn the wardrobe into a magical doorway."

Esmelia was impressed, despite her views on magic. The Fantastical Portal was a famously difficult spell. It could easily go wrong in ways that left people lost forever in other worlds, usually in very small chunks. Either that or it could take you places where you'd be forced to hold hands with fauns and forest folk then dance beneath the stars singing *fa la la la la*, which was even more horrible. Even history's greatest witches had thought twice before attempting Gammer Widdle's Fantastical Portal, and only then when there was no other choice. Esmelia thought about telling Sam to be careful, then caught herself and shrugged. It wasn't *her* lookout if the little twerp got herself chunked.

Sam stood in front of the room's carved, old wardrobe with Ringo on her shoulder. Girl and beetle made complicated patterns in the air with wand and legs and Sam chanted. The words took on colour as they left her mouth, and became tiny balls of magic that streamed around and into the wardrobe. Slowly the magic built and built until with a fierce golden flare it disappeared, leaving the wardrobe looking like just like the normal piece of furniture it had been ten minutes before.

Slipping her wand into a back pocket, Sam turned to Esmelia. "I won't be long," she said grimly. "Take care of Cakula." Then she walked through the open doors and between the heavy fur coats that always turn up in magical wardrobes. There was a glint of gold and she disappeared.

Rubbing her hands together in glee, Esmelia got up out of the armchair and loomed as only a witch can loom. Her shadow crept across the bed. "Oh yes dearie, I'll take care of *her* alright," she crowed. Skeleton thin fingers reached out and grasped the frog. "You and me is going for a little walk Croakula von Duckpond…" she cackled.

There was a lake just down the road from the Goblin's Elbow. Esmelia had spotted it glimmering in the moonlight as they had flown in. Now, she slipped The Most Superior High and Wicked Witch into its cold waters, murmuring, "I'm sure you'll be very wet and slimy here. You likes a bit of wet and slimy don't you, you froggies?"

As Cakula swam down the mud at the bottom of the lake, Esmelia's hand darted out like a lasso and caught a different frog – which had been sitting in some reeds minding its own business – round the throat. "Ribb… uuurgh" it choked as she held it up in the moonlight.

One frog looks very much like another, a fact that hadn't escaped Esmelia's notice. "You'll do," she muttered, turning the poor creature this way and that. "Congratulations Mr Frog, you've just been promoted. You're now Most Superior High and Wicked Witch. What do you think of that, eh?"

Judging by its furiously kicking legs, the frog wasn't too impressed. Esmelia stuffed it head first into a pocket and turned back to the warm lights of the Goblin's Elbow. "Oooo, I can't wait to see the little maggot's face when she tries to turn *you* back," she chuckled patting

her squirming pocket. "I told her old Esmelia's got a few tricks up her vest, but they don't listen do they, the young people?"

The tiny part of Esmelia that had wanted to pat Sam on the head really was a very tiny part indeed. Still cackling, the wicked witch strolled off towards the inn. She was in a very good mood indeed. *Maybe*, she thought, *she should pop into the bar for a little drinkie.*

9 The Most Superior High and Wicked Witch (Acting)

"I got a second-hand botty, you can use it as a hat, and if you leans right over, then I'm goin' to kick *that*," sang Esmelia in her sleep. Sam reached over and shook her by the shoulder. "Eh? Eh? You've been a lovely audience… thankyouverymuch goodnight," cried the old witch, shaking Sam's hand off and rolling over.

"Esmelia. *Esmelia*! It's morning. Diabolica will be looking for us. We can't stay here."

One of Esmelia's eyes opened. She looked up into the pale face of her apprentice. Sam looked grim. And alone. Her eyes were red, as if she'd been crying again.

"Dobblyolica got to the potions girl first then?" grunted the old witch, sitting up in bed and opening the other eye, which made a small popping sound.

"I don't know," replied her apprentice quietly, her voice catching a little. "There was just an empty shop."

Esmelia pulled the covers up to her bearded chin and sank back into the pillows. Her memories of the night before were a bit fuzzy. There had been wizards, she was sure. And singing. Singing seemed like something that might have happened. "How awful," she grumped in reply to Sam, before rolling over and closing her eyes again. "But not as awful as what'll happen to you if you wakes me up again."

"If we aren't out of the room soon, Mr Ulcer says he's going to make you pay for another day."

Twenty seconds later, Esmelia strode into the bar with Sam behind her. A small group of red-nosed, hairy-eared wizards were huddled over a newspaper at a table in the corner. Two of them had beards so enormous it looked like someone had stapled sheep to their faces, and all of them had tall hats, spangled with stars that bobbed as the wizards nodded together.

"I told you something bad is a-coming," muttered Professor Sebastian Dentrifice, jabbing a thick, potion-stained finger at the paper. "I saw it in the mystick thingummybobs."

"Are you sure?" said the younger, beardless wizard, who was called Wolfbang Pigsibling.

"No, he's right," interrupted Old Harry "Wooden" Legg. "Something wicked is this way a-coming. Last night one o' me legs fell right off. That's a sign, that is. You knows what they say: 'Lose an arm and you'll come to no harm, but if a leg goes astray somethin' wicked is comin' your way.'"

Old Harry fumbled with a strap under the table. With a clonk a wooden leg fell out from under his robe and rolled towards the fire. "There it goes again," he whispered. "'Tis evil afoot."

Professor Dentrifice rolled his eyes in disgust, then looked up and spotted Esmelia, "Mornin' Esnojeffreybumser," he boomed. "Seen the paper? Something bad a-comin' we reckon. It's them darned witches again."

He passed Esmelia up a copy of *The Cackler*, chuckling, "Witches, eh? Can't live with 'em, can't burn 'em at the stake."

"Yeah you can," Wolfbang cut it. "They burn really well does witches. Famous for it."

Sam and Esmelia craned their heads over the newspaper. "CAKULA MISSING!" the headline screamed. Underneath, it read "Witching World in Chaos!" then, in smaller letters, "Diabolica Nightshade says: 'Time Right For World Domination!'"

Esmelia's lips moved silently as she read the article.

The Cackler *has learned that Most Superior High and*

Wicked Witch Cakula von Drakula has vanished from the Bleak Fortress, leaving the witching world without a leader.

The shocking news was broken by Diabolica Nightshade who, until now, has been in hiding after her recent naughtiness. Diabolica said, "I have been unfairly treated by Cakula and went to the Bleak Fortress to reason with her. Poisoning Old Biddy Vicious, cheating at the trials for Most Superior High and Wicked Witch, and trying to kill some other witches were just pranks, simple high spirits. Which witch hasn't gotten a bit carried away with the poison bottle or hatched a dastardly plot now and again? Should we be treated as criminals just for acting like witches? I, for one, don't think so. So I went to see The Most Superior High and Wicked Witch to ask her to call off this ridiculous witch-hunt. Imagine my total and utter surprise – no really – to find the Bleak Fortress completely empty. What sort of Most Superior High and Wicked Witch just wanders off without telling anyone or even leaving a note? Really, witches deserve more from their leader."

The self-confessed power-crazed evil sorceress out to take over the world, added, "But if that crazy old vampire has decided to desert her post, it seems to me that it would be an excellent time for all decent and proper witches to get together for a bit of total world domination. Who's with me?"

In The Cackler's *opinion there has been foul play at the Bleak Fortress, and Diabolica Nightshade is almost certainly behind it. Under the Witching Law, in the absence of the Most Superior High and Wicked Witch whoever came second last time should be called upon to step up to the top job until a new trial can be organised. Unfortunately that was Esmelia Sniff, so everyone should probably ignore that rule. In the meantime, Diabolica has called for a general meeting of witches in Transylvania tonight, where she will unveil her plans for world domination.*

The Cackler *will, of course, be there to report.*

Esmelia's mouth fell open. She was the official acting Most Superior High and Wicked Witch. At least until Cakula returned, which would be never. The newspaper slipped between her fingers and fell to the floor.

"It's a bad business alright, Esnojeffreybumser," boomed Professor Dentrifice, mistaking the look on Esmelia' face as one of alarm and slapping her on the back. "Those blooming witches are *always* causing trouble. Best to stay here and have another sing-song, eh? Let the ladies get on with plunging the world into a pit of pain and despair or whatever gets into their fluffy little heads."

To Sam's amazement, Esmelia didn't poke the wizard in the eye. She was too flabbergasted even for that. Her lips moved. "Most Superior High and Wicked Witch," she breathed quietly. "That's me, that is."

For a few seconds she didn't do anything but stare into the distance with her jaw around her knees. Then, she pulled herself together. She punched the wizard on the arm, which for anyone else would have been a friendly gesture but – because it was Esmelia – left Professor Dentrifice with a bruise that would last for weeks, then barked, "I'd love to stay Sebastian old chap, but you knows what us wizards is like. Got to be sticking our big noses in the mystical whatnots, prodding at things-what-man-is-not-supposed-to-muck-about-with and generally making a nuisance of ourselves, eh?"

In her wildest dreams, Sam had never imagined that *anyone* might actually *want* to spend time with Esmelia, but the wizard seemed almost upset, "What a shame, what a shame," he murmured. "Not often you meet such a decent chap. What was that little ditty you taught us last night, 'I'm Kicking Your Bum Because it's Fabulous Fun,' was it? Marvellous. Simply marvellous… I haven't laughed so much since young Pigsibling here got trapped in a jam jar with a Gobbler Demon. Apprentices, eh? Useless bunch of twonks. Not like in *our* day."

Beneath the beard, Esmelia's mouth twitched. For a brief, fleeting moment, Sam thought the old witch might smile. Then the twitch had gone. "Come on you gawping little maggo... errr... useless little twonk," Esmelia muttered, gripping her apprentice by the shoulder. Sam found herself being pushed her towards the door, with just a short stop while Esmelia stuffed her pockets and vest with sausages and bacon from the breakfast trays. "Fifty-eight pee is fifty-eight pee," she mumbled. "Gotta get me money's worth." Just to make sure, she also helped herself to a handful of spoons.

When the two witches had left, Professor Dentrifice sat back down at the table. "Remarkable fellow," he said to no one in particular. "Very interesting chap."

"There was something odd about him though," grumbled Old Harry. "Did you notice his beard?"

Professor Sebastian Dentrifice stroked his own magnificent set of whiskers for a moment, then said slowly, "It was a little bit on the small side wasn't it?"

10 Mandy Snoutley Investigates

Mandy Snoutley looked like a fish that had been beaten with the ugly stick. A fish that had then been squeezed into a dress three sizes too small for it. A fish that was wearing a moth-eaten blonde wig that resembled a frightened candyfloss on its head. But Diabolica Nightshade had chosen Mandy as her henchperson for a very good reason. Beneath Mandy's wig was a vicious, spiteful mind that weaseled away secrets and gossip and interesting snippets of information that people would really rather were forgotten about thankyouverymuch. It's amazing how often knowing those sorts of things comes in handy for evil sorceresses like Diabolica.

Mandy Snoutley was, in fact, very *very* good at finding things out. And when she'd found something out, she was also very good at using what she'd found out to make people squirm.

She had started by reading back through police reports on missing persons. This had led her to a small town close to Esmelia's burned cottage, then to a library where she had flicked through old copies of the local newspapers.

Finally, Mandy found what she was looking for: a photograph and an address.

An hour later, Mandy Snoutley was sitting in the office of an orphanage squinting at the flustered woman across the untidy desk. Mandy had taken off her pointed hat in the hope that she would be mistaken for an everyday, run-of-the-mill, normal person, but it hadn't really worked. She just looked like a completely mad and probably dangerous old woman rather than a completely mad and probably dangerous old witch.

Ms Jane Spinnycott, who was the manager of the orphanage from which Sam had run away three months ago, sat and stared, boggle-eyed, at the strange woman opposite. On the desk in front of her was a large folder, which she fiddled with nervously. Realizing that she was being rude, Ms Spinnycott coughed to cover her embarrassment. "So," she said at last. "You think you might be related to our Samantha, I understand?"

"Yes, that's right. I'm her aunt, aren't I? Dear Aunty Mandy, that's me. Oh yes."

Ms Spinnycott made a tiny "Pffffff" noise of disbelief. She remembered Sam as a pretty girl, though one who always looked as though she needed a bath even after she'd just had a bath. *This* hideous creature looked as if her closest relatives scuttled about in mud at the bottom of the sea. "I see," she eventually managed to croak. "Well, Samantha was with us since she was a tiny baby. May I ask why you've never come to find her before?"

Mandy shuffled in her chair and plucked at her wig, which has slipped over one eye. Normally it was her asking the questions. It felt all wrong having to *answer* them. "No," she said. "You can't."

"Oh. Well have you got any proof?"

"Eh? Proof? What *are* you gabbling on about?"

"Proof that you're related. A birth certificate perhaps? Papers... documents."

Mandy winked, causing a fresh shiver of horror to run down Miss Spinnycott's spine. "I know what sort of papers you're after," she said, rummaging about in her handbag. After pulling out more make-up than you'd find in a stage school dressing room, a small crossbow and a foul-smelling sock, Mandy Snoutley held out a £50 note. "Will this do?" she asked.

"Bribery! I'm calling the police," Ms Spinnycott shouted, her hand already reaching for the telephone. "You're one of those awful *reporters* aren't you? I knew it as soon as I saw you."

"I *used* to be an awful reporter dearie, but now I'm just an evil henchperson," Mandy sighed. She hated dealing with non-witches. Although she went out of her way to look normal, just like them, she always ended up having to use the magic. There being nothing else for it, Mandy muttered a few words and clicked her fingers.

Instantly, Jane Spinnycott dropped the phone. "Dear Aunty Mandy," she giggled. "How *wonderful* of you to come. Let me tell you *all* about your delightful niece. *Such* a shock when she ran away. Anything I can do to help find her, please just ask."

"That's more like it," grinned Mandy, putting her feet up. "You can start by telling me everything you know about where she came from. Were her family from around these parts?"

"Oh no," said Jane Spinnycott in a voice that sounded like she was dreaming. "We got her when she was about a month old, but she was brought here from an orphanage in Scotland that burned down. All the children were sent to different homes and we were lucky enough to get Samantha."

Mandy swore. It looked like she was going to have to go to all the way to Scotland to continue her investigation. But Ms Spinnycott wasn't finished.

"Funny," she twinkled, opening the file.

"The orphanage in Scotland said she was just left of the doorstep. You get that from time to time, of course, but Samantha was holding onto *this* as if her little life depended on it."

THE WHITE WAND

Jane Spinnycott opened the file and held up an old branch. A few grey leaves and some dark, squashed, berries still clung to it. "It took them hours to get it out of her hand and she was only a day old."

Mandy leaned forward for a better look. She wasn't the type of witch that bothered with herbs and plants, but there was something about the dried branch that stirred her memory. She'd seen it a long time ago, back

when she'd been an apprentice.

"I took the trouble of looking it up in a book when Samantha first arrived," continued Ms Spinnycott. "It's a poisonous plant. In the olden days they used to call it belladonna – which means 'beautiful lady' – or some people called it 'dwale'. These days, most people know it as…"

"…Deadly Nightshade," whispered Mandy.

Ordinarily, Mandy Snoutly was not the type of person who went pale, or got goosebumps, or shouted, "Oh my aunt Fanny's sainted pineapple!" Ordinarily, she was the *reason* that people did those things. Now, however, she did all three. The plot hadn't just thickened, it had gone all sticky with lumpy bits in.

11 Sam & Esmelia Undercover

Sam and Esmelia circled the Bleak Fortress. The storm had blown itself out, leaving the castle under a thick duvet of snow that sparkled beneath the soft moonlight and lights that blazed from the fortress's windows. By the glow of flaming torches, Sam could see witches below. Hundreds of witches, all pouring across the courtyard and through the Great Entrance like pointy-hatted bees returning to the hive.

"I still don't think this is going to work," said Sam. She was wearing a fake nose that Esmelia had carved from a potato and tied on with string. Ringo was fussing over several acorns that he had stuck to her face to look like warts. Esmelia had also blackened most of Sam's teeth with a burned twig, smeared dirt on her face and pushed a bag filled with leaves up her sweater to give her a hunched back. It wasn't a very good disguise, but, as Esmelia explained, it wasn't unusual for witches to be so daft that they would stick nuts and potatoes to their faces or stuff leaves up their jumpers. What mattered was that no one recognized that it was Sam, the witch, disguised as a witch.

"Got a hunch have you?" cackled Esmelia, giving Sam's leafy back a slap and making the hump slip down to her waist.

Sam pushed it back up between her shoulders. "What about your beard?" she asked. "You can't go to a meeting of witches with a beard as a disguise. They'll spot it straight away."

"Don't you be worryin' about that," replied Esmelia, stroking her beard. "There's been quite a few beardy witches. Dame Peggy Bristle used to have to shave with an electric hedge trimmer and Old Hetty 'The Yeti' Gitspewington was so hairy she once got mistaken for a haystack... At least, that's what the farmer who stuck a pitchfork in her said."

Sam nodded. It was too late to argue now. They were here, and though her stomach felt like jelly and she had butterflies in her knees at the thought of coming face to face with Diabolica again, she had to admit she couldn't think of a better plan than Esmelia's.

"Remember," the old witch continued, poking Sam's shoulder. "We sneaks in, then hides in a dark corridor round the back. When the meeting's over I'll jump out on Dumbellica and while I pokes her in the eye and twiddles me finger about, you grabs the wand. Then I'll give her the knee, on account of how she burned me cottage down. And after that I'll pull her arms off and slowly…"

"No! There won't be time for that. As soon as we've got the wand we make our getaway and find somewhere safe where we can change Cakula back. That's the plan. Alright?"

If Sam had looked behind her, she might have seen a wicked glint in Esmelia's eye. "Oh, I ain't forgotten about *that*," the old witch crowed, "I bin looking forward to it."

In the Throne Room of the Bleak Fortress a stage had been set up with the throne of the Most Superior High and Wicked Witch in the centre. Before the stage was a bubbling cauldron, lit by red spotlights. Thick black smoke poured over the sides and coiled round the ankles of hundreds of muttering witches.

As Sam and Esmelia jostled their way into the crowd a hag whose face looked like a bowl of cherries and custard, moaned, "Should have been at home squeezing me boils tonight." Another crossed her arms and grumbled to anyone who'd listen, "That Nightshade baggage better not be wasting my time, Tuesday night is the night I play bingo with the spawn of the dark pit. I made sandwiches and everything." One worried voice squeaked, "You know Beryl, I don't think this *is* the right place for Randy Stardust and The Swinging Wowzers."

Sam was surprised to find that Esmelia had been right. If anyone had noticed her awful disguise, they clearly didn't think it was worth mentioning. Even so, as she followed Esmelia through the crowd, she kept the brim of her hat pulled down.

Suddenly, the lights blinked out, plunging the room into darkness for a heartbeat, then spotlights flared into life, criss-crossing the room with red beams before settling on the stage. Diabolica had appeared. Draped over the throne as if it were the squishiest of soft sofas, and slowly tapping the The Black Wand of Ohh Please Don't Turn Me Into Aaaarghh… Ribbett against her cheek, she was wearing a tight, black gown that shimmered under the lights. Her hair fell to her waist in shining coils and for the first time, Sam saw she was wearing the traditional witch's pointy black hat. Only, it wasn't a pointy black hat like any she'd seen before. Tall, elegant, and set with rare black rubies, it made every other hat in the room look like it had been made from dishcloths by one-armed monkeys. Behind her stood a wall of blank faced, unblinking witches.

Diabolica Nightshade dripped with style.

"*There*. That's where she come out of," hissed Esmelia into Sam's ear. The apprentice tore her eyes off the stage and peered into the shadows where Esmelia was pointing. To the side of the stage was a small, dark doorway. Slowly, the two witches began to edge towards it.

Around them, the crowd was already turning nasty, which, of course, was no big surprise. With any crowd of witches, or even witches who are quite alone, nastiness comes as standard.

"Get on with it then," called a voice from the back.

"Where's Cakula, eh? Vampires don't just vanish into thin air in a puff of smoke… Oh, they *do* do that though, don't they? Sorry, don't mind me."

"Oooo, she's got the wand!" cried a witch at the front, "She's only gone and pinched The Black Wand of Ohh Please Don't Turn Me Into Aaaarghh… Ribbett."

"Who does she think she is? Most Superior High and Wicked Witch?" yelled another.

"No, *officially* that's Esmelia Sniff," called Esmelia Sniff, then ducked.

Sam glared at Esmelia. "We're supposed to be sneaking," she hissed.

Another witch joined in the shouting. "Since we're all here, the first thing we should agree is that we'd rather have a bag of toenails as Most Superior High and Wicked Witch than Esmelia Sniff," she cried.

A rumble of approval rolled around the huge room. The witch next to Esmelia began clapping, but stopped when she got a sharp elbow to the stomach.

"Ouch," the witch screeched. "What d'you do that for, beard-face?"

"Got a twitch in me elbow," explained Esmelia. "Look, there it goes again."

"Aaargh." The clapping witch doubled over in pain.

Sam sighed and pushed Esmelia away. They were getting closer to the doorway now. Around them, witches continued shouting at Diabolica.

"Look, that's Ophelia Pane behind her," screeched one, pointing at a witch in Diabolica's army. "She went missing a couple of days ago.

And Geraldine Squirtblaster. Why're they standing there like drooling idiots? Diabolica's magicked them into zombies or something." "I hate witches what goes around stealing The Black Wand of Ohh Please Don't Turn Me Into Aaaarghh… Ribbett, bumping off the Most Superior High and

Wicked Witch, and making me miss me TV shows," grumped yet another. "Plus, her face gets on me nerves. Let's scrag her."

"Yeah. Give her a walloping."

"Pulverize the pert trollop."

"And after that let's *really* give her a kicking."

Diabolica's secretive smile didn't flicker. Slowly, she raised her hand, and the crowd of witches grumbled a little more quietly, so that Sam could hear a whisper from the front, "No Beryl, it's not Randy Stardust, I think it's Shirley Diamond and the Zombie Crone Choir."

Under the unblinking green gaze of Diabolica's eyes, the crowd of witches at last grew silent. "Well, hello there," she purred. "And welcome to a whole new world."

12 Diabolica's Army

Beneath the gruesome carved ceiling of the Bleak Fortress's throne room, Diabolica began to talk. Followed by red spotlights, she strutted across the stage and told her audience how powerful they could be if they would only join together. The crowd grew silent as she pointed out that witches had been hunted down and burned at the stake throughout history; pointed, jeered and laughed at, or forced to earn a living making up rubbish horoscopes for the newspapers. She reminded them of all the stories where witches are pushed in their own ovens, or have their heads chopped off by woodcutters, or are crushed to death by falling houses. Every so often she reached into a bag at the side of the stage and threw glittering dust into the cauldron. The spotlights dimmed and the smoke grew darker and darker as Diabolica spoke of a world ruled by witches.

"We are the wise women," she told her silent audience. "Blessed with the gift of magic. Why do we stay in the shadows? Why do we live in tumbledown shacks in forests? What are we hiding from?"

"I'm hiding from the milkman," called a voice in

the crowd. "I owe him a hundred and forty-six pounds and twenty pee."

A snigger ran around the crowd.

Diabolica walked to the front of the stage with her hands on her hips and stared at the witch who had spoken. In a quiet voice she said, "Why *pay*? You're a *witch*, aren't you?"

As the witch scowled at her, Diabolica sat in the throne with her chin in her hands and stared out across the sea of pointy hats. "It seems to me," she whispered, and every ear strained to hear, "that a world with witches in charge would be a *better* world. A world of excitement and wild magic. A world where we could, at last, be great."

Speaking slowly, as if the idea had just occurred to her, she went on, "So, what if we created an army of witches? With The Black Wand of Ohh Please Don't Turn Me Into Aaaarghh... Ribbett and all our mystic knowledge and magic..." She paused for a few seconds, then finished quietly, "The whole world would soon be at our feet, where it belongs."

"I don't think the world would like that," muttered a witch close to Sam. "I got athlete's foot something terrible. And bunions, verrucas and the manky hoof."

There was complete silence in the throne room. Black smoke twisted and curled around every witch, and Sam and Esmelia were the only ones moving. Inch by inch they were getting closer to the doorway and a dark corridor where they could lay in wait to ambush Diabolica.

Eventually, a witch coughed, "that's all very well dearie, but after we've done all that we all know what happens next, don't we?"

"Yup," said another. "Next you'd want to be queen then, isn't it? I know your type."

"We all know *her* type," screeched a witch near the front. "They ain't happy unless they're queening about the place bein' all terrible and beautiful and, frankly, a right pain in the bum."

"*And* she'll probably be making it winter *all the time*. They always do. I *hate* winter. It plays merry hell with me rheumatism."

"And excuse me, but if we was to join a witch army that'd mean spending a lot more time with other witches, wouldn't it? I can't *bear* other witches. Bunch of miserable, trout-faced old ratbags your witches... Except me. That goes without saying."

There was murmur of agreement. "Aye, she's not

wrong there. I *really* hates them witches," said a witch.

"Anyway, I can't be joinin' no army," hissed a hag. "I'm washing me hair next week."

For a moment there was absolute silence again, except for the sound of hundreds of witches gasping, then the last witch cackled, "Nah, not *really*, I'm just pullin' yer legs."

The Great Hall of the Bleak Fortress descended into chaos. Sam and Esmelia edged another couple of feet nearer to the door.

"What's she got against living in forests anyway? It's *healthy* is living in the forest and you got all the squirrels you can eat, right there on your doorstep."

"Can we start the scragging now?"

Diabolica held up her hand for quiet just as someone yelled, "I'd like to see the day when I takes orders from a skinny ninny in a sparkly hat and silly shoes."

"You would, would you?" smiled Diabolica. "Well, luckily for you I just *knew* you bunch of stupid cauldron-bothering bat-fanciers might kick up a fuss, so I've taken steps."

She paused again. Around the room, the cauldron-bothering bat-fanciers peered at each other in confusion.

Then Diabolica continued, "You see, I wasn't exactly *asking* you to join my army. It was more like *telling* you, really, though if it makes you feel better, you were right about the whole queen thing. When I said the world will be at *our* feet, I meant, of course, *my* feet." She threw one last handful of glittery dust into the cauldron, then stirred it in with The Black Wand of Ohh Please Don't Turn Me Into Aaaarghh... Ribbett.

Sam and Esmelia dashed the last couple of yards towards the door, but it was too late. An evil black cloud of smoke burst from the cauldron and flooded into every corner of the Great Hall. For a few moments the vast room echoed with curses and spluttered coughs. Then, in the gloom, a witch spoke, in a chilling voice that sounded as though it had come straight from the grave.

"Di-a-bol-i-ca," she droned.

The voice in the darkness was joined by another, just as dead-sounding. "Di-a-bol-i-ca. Di-a-bol-i-*ca*." Another, then another and another began, until the Great Hall was filled with chanting voices.

Sam stood stiffly in the darkness. She opened her mouth, and moaned "Di-a-bol-i-ca" along with the crowd. On her shoulder, Ringo jumped up and down, pinched her with his pincers and punched her in the ear.

Sam didn't flinch. She no longer cared about anything other than the beautiful witch on stage. Her queen.

Esmelia, too, stared forward, seeing nothing. Her eyes were unblinking and all plans forgotten. *Everything* was forgotten; everything except Diabolica, for whom Esmelia would now throw herself into a nest of angry wasps.

The chanting reached a peak. "Di-a-bol-i-ca," "Di-a-bol-i-ca," the witches groaned, until the evil sorceress held up her hand again. At once, all noise stopped.

"Believe me," she giggled, "you won't miss your minds. It's not as if you were using them. I mean, did you really think I had a bubbling cauldron on stage just for the look of it? For badness sake, you really *are* a bunch of stupid crones."

While Diabolica howled with triumphant laughter, hands reached out in the darkness and took Sam and Esmelia by their elbows. By the time the black cloud had cleared, the hands had pulled them through the crowd towards the main doors and into the corridor that led to the courtyard.

13 Escape From the Bleak Fortress

"Oh, like *totally*, drat and that," said a young witch with purple hair. Safe in the snowy courtyard she plucked the potato and acorns off Sam's face and looked her and Esmelia up and down. They seemed to be staring at something a thousand miles away and their mouths were opening and shutting, making them both look like particularly brainless fishes. For a moment, the young witch wondered why Esmelia was wearing a false beard, before continuing to rummage around the inside of her coat until she found a bottle of black liquid and a spoon. Carefully, she measured out a drop and slipped it into Sam's mouth, then did the same for Esmelia.

The two witches' faces turned blue. They clutched at their throats as the potion burned its way down.

"Wark" yelled Esmelia, her eyes bulging. "Di-a-boooo! Hot. *Hot*. Must. Eat. Penguins…"

"Good grief, what is that?" gasped Sam. "It feels like my head's going to explode."

"Mmm, that'll be the gunpowder."

"Helza!" cried Sam, leaping forward and hugging her friend. "I thought Diabolica had caught you." Tears sprang to her eyes, and not just because of the gunpowder.

"Not me," grinned Helza Poppin, hugging Sam back. "Wisteria Wickham is, like, *awesome* with a crystal ball. She saw Diabolica coming from miles off."

Sam and Helza hugged each other hard and didn't hear the soft crunch of feet in the snow. "What a very *touching* scene," said a voice behind them. The two girls let each other go, and whirled round to see Diabolica standing on the steps to the Great Entrance, dabbing at her eyes with a handkerchief. Zombie witches shuffled past her.

"Oooo, that's good stuff that is," spluttered Esmelia at last. "That'd go nice in a curry." She looked up, saw Diabolica, and remembered where she was. "Oh, it's the cottage burner-downerer," she said flatly. "Now, where did I put that finger? Oh yes, here it is."

Without warning, Esmelia threw herself at Diabolica, who simply stepped aside, Two large zombie witches caught the old witch and twisted her arms up behind her back.

"Oi! Watch it!" Esmelia screeched. "I'm a poor,

feeble old lady, I am."

Sam whistled for her broom. Nothing happened.

"I *knew* you'd all come," smiled Diabolica, ignoring Esmelia and taking a step closer. "It was hilarious watching you trying to hide in the crowd. I hope you don't mind, but I had shuffling mindless thing number fifteen find your broom, Sam." She pointed to where an empty-faced witch was wrestling with Sam's thrashing broom. "It wasn't difficult. Such *interesting* magic in it. Did Lilith Dwale make it? She's been helping you through that book, too, hasn't she? Who *is* she?"

Sam ignored the questions and raised her wand. Diabolica sneered, "Oh put that down. You know you're no match for me and The Black Wand of Ohh Please Don't Turn Me Into Aaaarghh… Ribbett. And this time I've made sure there will be no escape spells either."

Wearily, Sam lowered the wand and shrugged at her friend, whispering, "Thanks anyway, Helza. It was nice of you to try."

"Nil problemo, bud," replied Helza. "Any time."

Diabolica took another step closer, snow crunching beneath her totteringly high heels, and put out a hand to touch Helza's face. "*Igor*," she said sweetly. "After I've sucked your mind out, I think I'll make you my servant again. Only until I've thought of some especially horrible fate for you, but for a little while at least."

Helza jerked her head away from Diabolica's hand. "What*ever*," she snapped. And she meant it to sting.

Diabolica giggled. "Anyway, can't stand here chatting all day. Worlds don't just take over themselves you know, but I've got all kinds of surprises in store for you." She crooked a finger, and ordered, "Dungeons first I think. And would one of you zombie things kindly get the hot thumbscrews ready…"

Esmelia had had enough. She scowled at the two witches holding her. "You got me arms nice and tight?" she asked. They nodded slowly. "That's nice," Esmelia continued. "Forgot about me feet though, didn't you?"

What the two witches had also forgotten was that though Esmelia wasn't good at much, she was an expert when it came to fighting. Many a witch who'd come away from a jumble sale with a black eye and bleeding ears could have told them that.

Two sturdy boots lashed out and caught both witches right on the kneecaps. They went down screaming "Di-a-bol-i-caaaarrrgggghHHH."

"Tiddles!" yelled Esmelia. "*Kill!*"

Esmelia's black cat shot through the crowd, clawed

his way up the dress of the witch holding Sam's broom and hurled himself in a hissing, spitting fury of claws onto her head. The zombie-witch cried our in pain, and whirled about, letting go of the broom and clutching at the furious cat. Tiddles sank his teeth into her fingers and continued scratching great gashes across her face.

Diabolica raised The Black Wand of Ohh Please Don't Turn Me Into Aaaarghh… Ribbett, but now it was Ringo's turn. The beetle launched himself in a flurry of wings right into her face.

A beetle might not sound like the most terrible of attackers, but Ringo was a bigger beetle than most. With any insect attack there is also the 'yuk' factor to deal with. Even a power-crazed, evil sorceress hates having a bug buzzing around her head.

"Ewwww," Diabolica shrieked, flapping at the beetle and taking a hasty step back, at which point she learned a valuable lesson in sensible footwear. Her heels slipped on the snow and Diabolica fell backwards, dropping The Black Wand of Ohh Please Don't Turn Me Into Aaaarghh… Ribbett as she put her hands out to break the fall.

Three things happened at once. Esmelia grabbed Tiddles and leapt at The Black Wand of Ohh Please

Don't Turn Me Into Aaaarghh… Ribbett. Sam whistled. Helza punched the air and yelled, "Go Ringo! In your *face*, Diabolica."

In the confusion all three witches threw themselves on Sam's broom. It wooshed into the night sky like a rocket.

Below, Diabolica was already screeching, "Oh no, not *again*. Spells, you fools! STOP THEM!"

Sam, Helza, and Esmelia were flung, squealing, this way and that as the broom climbed and dodged spells. At the front, Sam managed to balance herself looking backwards. Quickly, she whipped her wand around, countering spell after spell. Esmelia was perched on the twiggy end, holding up The Black Wand of Ohh Please Don't Turn Me Into Aaaarghh… Ribbett and cackling in glee. Below them, Helza clung to the underside of the broom, shouting "waaaaaah" at the top of her lungs. Tiddles tried to make himself comfy on her stomach and Ringo jumped up and down on Sam's hat making rude gestures at the witches on the ground below. The spells of a thousand witches burst, sizzled, and popped around them but, even with three witches on board, the broom was moving fast. After a few moments, Sam stopped casting counter spells long enough to shout, "You were

brilliant Esmelia! We did it!"

"I told you I had a few tricks up me vest," the old witch cackled back. "Maybe next time you'll believe me when I tells you a good trick is betterer than all that hokey pokey stuff..."

A fireball screamed out of the sky behind them and caught Esmelia on the fingertips. "Ow ow ow ow, blast, drat, and did I mention OWWWW!" she screeched, sucking her smoking fingers.

Then, as she watched The Black Wand of Ohh Please Don't Turn Me Into Aaaarghh... Ribbett falling back towards Diabolica below, she added, "Oh *bum*."

Sam gaped at Esmelia, lost for words. Another fireball zizzed out of the night sky, and this time caught the broom in its tail twigs. They burst into flame. The broom spiralled away from the Bleak Fortress trailing smoke and carrying three screaming witches, one of them flapping at a fire with her skirt.

14 Weird Séance

Sam had flown to the safest place she could think of. It had been a long and difficult journey with the damaged broomstick twisting crazily through the air. Now they were hunched, shivering, over the kitchen table of Blanche Nightly, Ghost Hunter, who lived in the empty and crumbling American town of Sawyer Bottom, hidden deep within thick forest.

"So," said Sam, as cheerfully as she could manage. "Diabolica is planning to take over the world. She has the Bleak Fortress, a thousand witches helping her, and the most powerful wand ever made. She's also planning to torture us all and then kill us… But at least we have the *official* Most Superior High and Wicked Witch, otherwise known as 'butterfingers' Sniff, on our side."

"Oi, you're still my apprentice, so watch your cheek," grumped Esmelia. "Anyway, it weren't my fault I dropped the wand. Blinkin' fireballs. Caught me best finger and all. It'll be ages before it's fit for pokin' again."

"Sam's right," said Helza. "We're going to need help. I can fetch Wisteria Wickham. She went back to the shop to make sure Diabolica hadn't stolen anything, but that's still only four of us against an army."

"Five of us dear," interrupted Blanche Nightly. The tubby ghost hunter set a teapot in the middle of the table. "You can count me in, too. Plus a lot of spirit people. There's been complaints about this Diabolica person in the world beyond. She's messin' about with dark magic and stuff when she shouldn't."

"Bah! Ghosts. What good is ghosts?" sniffed Esmelia. "What are they going to do? Go 'boo' at her? Oh yes, I daresay that'll stop her *right* in her tracks."

Blanche ignored her. "The spirits can help in many ways," she continued. "There are things known to them that have been forgotten in the world of the living. We should try speaking to them. But first of all, you all look as though you could do with a rest. Look, Sam's fallen asleep on her toast."

By the way, who's this little guy?" Helza asked, pointing at the frog that was sat on the table wondering what on Earth was going on.

"Oh, that's just Cakula von Drakula," cackled Esmelia. "Only she's all frogged up at the moment, ain't you, your Most Superior High and Wicked Vampireness?"

"Ribbett."

"That's just her way of telling you to mind your own business, or she'll leap up and tear your throat right out…"

"How strange," said Blanche. "It looks like a *boy* frog to me."

Esmelia swept the frog off the table and into a pocket, muttering, "She's just a bit *confused* at the moment is all."

The four witches were sat around a gloomy table by the light of a single flickering candle, with their fingers touching. "I'm sorry," said Blanche Nightly. "I just can't seem to tune in properly tonight."

So far they had spoken to the spirits of someone called Elvis who kept insisting that he wasn't *really* dead, and the Ghost of Christmas Past. The second spirit had tried to take Esmelia on a journey through her life to show her the error of her wicked ways, but had floated away crying "Dat's nod subbosed to habben," when she punched him on his ghostly nose.

"Maybe we should try again tomorrow," shrugged Blanche.

Just then, the ghost of a slim and pretty witch ran through the cottage wall, glancing back over her shoulder. A witch that Sam had seen only once before, when she had been finding recommendations for the Most Superior High and Wicked Witch Trials, but a witch she had spoken to almost every day since.

Sam felt a surge of relief, and a tingle, as her grandmother's transparent hand briefly touched her on the shoulder. Then Lilith Dwale began talking:

"I'll have to make this quick. Diabolica knows I'm in the *Think Yourself Witch* book and is trying to force me to answer her questions. It's taking all my energy just to hide from her."

"*Think Yourself Witch*? You never mean that book Dribblybumlica pinched out me cottage, does you?" interrupted Esmelia. "You mean to say you've been hauntin' my bookshelf all this time? Ooo, you weren't watchin' when I licked that toad and had a funny turn last year, was you?"

Lilith smiled at the old witch, and said, "Don't worry, your secret's safe with me. I'll never tell *anyone* that you put your knickers on your head and spent the whole day drawing little faces on your warts."

"You dirty fibber," shrieked Esmelia. "I never did."

"You did too," said Lilith primly. "Remember you called one of them Mr Henderson P. Warty? He was your best wart, you told him."

"Shutupshutupshutup," squealed Esmelia.

Sam shushed her into silence. Esmelia carried on glaring at the wispy figure floating by the table.

"Lilith," said Blanche, "we seem to be in a spot of bother in the saving the world department. Don't suppose you can help, can you?"

Lilith Dwale bowed her head and spoke in a voice full of doom. "No one and nothing can stand against Diabolica Nightshade and The Black Wand of Ohh Please Don't Turn Me Into Aaaarghh… Ribbett. Even now a darkness is spreading from the Bleak Fortress. A darkness that will call things into the world that were banished long ago. Wraiths, ghouls, werewolves, banshees… Icky stuff."

"But there must be something we can do," cried Sam. "We can't just give up."

Raising her head, Lilith replied in the same doomy tone, "There is one hope, but it's nothing more than a whisper of a rumour of a myth of a legend that I read in an ancient book long ago…"

"Look," Sam interrupted, "if you haven't got long

gra... err, Lilith, would you mind cutting out the riddles and gloomy speeches. Just *tell* us would you?"

"I'm *trying* to create the proper mood," snapped Lilith. She caught Sam's look and sighed. "Oh alright. A long time ago there was a story among witches that The Black Wand of Ohh Please Don't Turn Me Into Aaaarghh... Ribbett was made by the first witch in Ancient Egypt. If you could find the spell and create another wand just as powerful then you might be able to defeat Diabolica."

Lilith paused for a moment, looked around the table, then added, "Luckily, Sam is more powerful than she knows. It should be possible for her to perform the spell."

Sam blushed, and asked, "So where do we look?"

Lilith shrugged. "The book said The Lost Valley of the Witches. Hundreds of witches have tried to find it but none have ever succeeded..." Suddenly, Lilith looked over her shoulder. "Uh-oh, Diabolica's coming back. Must dash. Good luck."

The spirit of Lilith Dwale winked at her granddaughter, and vanished.

There was silence for a few moments. "I'll get a packed lunch ready then, shall I?" asked Esmelia eventually. Her devious mind worked quickly. To be the *proper* Most Superior High and Wicked Witch she needed to get her hands on The Black Wand of Ohh Please Don't Turn Me Into Aaaarghh... Ribbett, but it didn't need to be the *actual* Black Wand of Ohh Please Don't Turn Me Into Aaaarghh... Ribbett. Any amazingly powerful black wand would be alright by her, just so long as she could befrogginate anyone who got in her way."

"I'm not so sure," murmured Blanche. "It might be a better idea to start an army of our own. If hundreds of witches have been looking for this spell for thousands of years, it's not likely we'll just trip over it. If it still exists at all, it could take years to find but there's bound to be some witches whose minds Diabolica didn't suck out. The old ones who couldn't get onto a broom, and a few like me who couldn't be bothered to go to her meeting."

Sam sat up straight, her eyes sparkling. "I think we should try and find the spell..." she began. The idea of creating a new black wand, her *own* black wand, had touched something deep inside her. She could barely sit on her chair or speak for excitement. "I-I-I... well I know I can..." She was cut short. In a flutter of beetle wings, Ringo took off from her shoulder and whizzed around the room. Dropping to the table, the beetle pushed over a cup. Then, using spilled tea, began drawing with his front legs.

"Hey, he's drawing a map of, like, Africa," said Helza at last. "Cool. Your beetle's *totally* smart Sam. What's that bit he's

pointing at?"

Four heads craned over the tea-drawing.

"That's interesting," said Blanche. "It's Egypt. Look you can see the River Nile and little pyramids. I wonder what it means."

Sam took a deep breath. She knew what it meant and, once again, her heart filled with gratitude for her little familiar. "It means," she said slowly. "That Ringo wants to go home."

15 Once Upon a Time...

Diabolica Nightshade sat on the Great Throne of The Most Superior High and Wicked Witch with *Think Yourself Witch* open on her lap and a deep scowl on her face. She tapped a page with The Black Wand of Ohh Please Don't Turn Me Into Aaaarghh… Ribbett, and said, "I want to know how to find the dreadful Sam girl. I know you're in there Lilith Dwale, and if you don't talk things will get *very* nasty for you."

With her free hand, Diabolica rattled a box of matches.

Nothing happened. Lilith Dwale was keeping quiet.

"Curses," spat Diabolica, throwing the book to the floor and standing up to pace the floor. "I don't need *you* anyway. Soon, I won't need *anyone*. Mwah ha ha – and all that."

At the far end of the hall, the door opened and a very ugly, but grinning, witch skipped into the room.

"Mandy!" crowed Diabolica. "You're back, and by the look on your face you've done well. What did you find out?"

Mandy Snoutley's grin became so wide that the top

half of her head almost flopped off. "Well, your naughtiness," she tittered. "I know where to find Sam's mother."

Diabolica clapped her hands together excitedly. "*Excellent* Mandy. Sam's mother will make the perfect bait in a trap. We'll kidnap the woman and put the thumbscrews on her. We'll stretch her on the rack, and push poisonous centipedes in her ears..."

"Oooo, I don't think you'll be wanting to do all that, your keeping-a-big-secretness."

Mandy hugged herself. She should have known, she told herself. If being a reporter for *The Cackler* had taught her one thing, it was that *everyone* had skeletons in their closets. With witches it was usually *actual* skeletons, but most of them had secrets too. And this one was a biggie. A secret so brain-twistingly enormous that Mandy was giddy with glee.

"*What*? Have you gone ma... even *more* mad... to speak to me like that?"

"Oh no, Diabolica, or, should I say..." Mandy hugged herself again, then finished "... *Susan*?"

Diabolica sank onto the throne. Her hands gripped the armrests, and it was a few moments before she managed to hiss, "*What* did you call me?"

Mandy sniggered. "Faithful old henchperson Mandy found out a little bit more than she bargained for. It's quite a story. Would you like to hear it?"

Diabolica was whiter than a television presenter's teeth and little beads of sweat had broken out on her forehead. She nodded.

"Then I'll begin. Are you sitting comfortably?" Without waiting for Diabolica to reply, Mandy continued. "Once upon a time there was a girl called Susan who lived in an orphanage in Scotland. She was a bad one, everyone said – and she believed in magic. One day, Susan vanished, at just about the same time as Old Morag McFilthy, who lived in the woods close by, took on an apprentice. Of course, we don't know much about her apprentice because Old Morag was poisoned and her cottage burned to the ground not long after."

Mandy stopped talking and leered at Diabolica. "How are you liking it so far?"

Sweat poured down Diabolica's face. "It's a very, uh... *interesting*... tale Mandy. But I don't see what it has to do with *me*."

"Hang on, I ain't got to the good bit yet... So, a couple of years after Susan had run away, the same orphanage found a baby on the doorstep. A little baby girl with a branch of deadly nightshade in her hand. Funny thing was, that a Mrs err... hang on I got it here somewhere."

Mandy took a notebook from a band in her hat and thumbed through the pages. "Oh yes, Mrs Nesbit. Well, Mrs Nesbit said she'd opened her curtains one night and seen *Susan* running through the streets the night before weeping over a little bundle... you remember Mrs Nesbit, don't you? She ran the village sweet shop."

Diabolica nodded. Mandy grinned. "So it *was* you!" she cried. "I found an old photo, but I couldn't be exactly sure. You've changed a lot, *Susan*."

Realizing that Mandy had tricked her, Diabolica hissed again. "How dare you. I'll..."

Mandy held up her hand for silence. "But I've got

such *good* news, Diabolica. A few weeks later, the
orphanage burned down, and the baby girl Susan had
dumped there was sent to a new place a long way away.
Quite close to Esmelia Sniff's cottage, in fact. Funny
thing is that the baby grew up to be mad about magic as
well, and ran away, just like her mammy before her.
Samantha they named her, but the lady at the orphanage
said she liked to be called Sam."

There was silence for a couple of minutes. Inside
her head, Diabolica gaped, gibbered, gasped and
goggled. She hadn't thought about the baby for *years* and
had been certain that no one would ever find out about
the girl. Mandy was right, she *had* been a wild one when
she was a young witch just learning the craft and she had
never been very good about following rules. But now she
was discovered. She had broken the first law of
witchcraft *and* the baby had grown up to be her greatest
enemy. Diabolica made a small tutting sound. It was all
sooo unfair. Her own daughter. Her *daughter*.

Diabolica's face didn't move, but the sweat was now
staining her dress and her fingers twitched around The
Black Wand of Ohh Please Don't Turn Me Into
Aaaarghh… Ribbett. Finally, Mandy said quietly, "So,
you probably won't be wanting to put the thumbscrews

on Sam's mum. Seeing as it's *you*."

At last, Diabolica felt able to speak. "What will it take to keep you quiet Mandy?" she whispered.

"Well, there won't be any more of this 'henchperson' rubbish for a start. Plus, I want to be young and beautiful again. And before you even *think* about poisoning me off, I've made lots of notes and put them in a safe place. If anything happens to me they go straight to *The Cackler* and everyone will know you broke the first law of witchcraft."

At last, Diabolica's face moved. An eyebrow was raised, her fingers began drumming on the throne's armrest and a small smile pulled at the corner of her mouth. Everything was going to be alright after all.

"But Mandy," Diabolica purred. "I *quite* forgot to tell you. While you were away I sort of sucked a lot of minds out. I'd have to check, but I think that everyone from *The Cackler* was here. And, you know, even if they found out I don't think anyone would really *mind* about me breaking a silly old rule. It's so difficult to care about much when you're a drooling, shuffling zombie thing."

She stood up, her smile widening and evil shining in her deep green eyes.

Mandy took a step back, her grin disappearing.

"Eek," she whispered.

Sparkles glittered along The Black Wand of Ohh Please Don't Turn Me Into Aaaarghh… Ribbett. "But don't worry Mandy, I won't poison you," Diabolica laughed.

"Oh thank you, thank you, your wonderful glossy loveliness," cried Mandy, sinking to her knees and kissing the toes of Diabolica's very expensive and ridiculously high shoes. "I was only joking. I'd never say a word. Your secret's safe with faithful henchperson Mandy."

Diabolica jerked her foot away from Mandy's mouth. "Don't *do* that," she hissed. "You'll get spit all over them." Then black light wrapped around Mandy Snoutley as The Black Wand of Ohh Please Don't Turn Me Into Aaaarghh… Ribbett did what it did best.

Trembling all over, Diabolica slumped back into the throne and watched as Mandy hopped away. She had never dreamed that the baby might grow up to be magical, but now she thought about it she supposed there must be a reason that witches weren't allowed to have children. Perhaps, she thought, magic could be passed down in families. That would explain why Sam was so powerful, too. As she cast her mind back,

Diabolica wondered why she hadn't guessed that Sam was her daughter before. Every time she had met the girl she had had a strange feeling, a bit like a ghost walking through her, or having jam in her shoes. It was the eyes, she realised. Looking into Sam's eyes was like looking into a mirror. And she had always thought that Sam would be pretty if someone took the trouble to wash the dirt off her...

After a few moments Diabolica stopped trembling and began smiling again. As an enemy, Sam was infuriating and dangerous but as a *daughter* she might prove to be very useful indeed. So long as she was completely under control of course.

"My little girl," she murmured. "Well, well, well..."

At her feet, unseen, the words in *Think Yourself Witch* finally changed.

Drat! wrote Diabolica's mother.

16 The Valley of The Witches

Sam sat on a rock with her chin in her hands while the sun was setting behind her in a glorious nosebleed of red and pink with streaks of gold. Dotted around the rocky valley below were pyramids and statues of women in tall hats with cats at their feet. Near Sam's rock was a stone pillar carved with the Ancient Egyptian picture writing. Using a book Blanche had lent her, called *Get By in Ancient Egyptian in Just One Week!*, Sam had tried to make sense of it. As far as she could tell, the pictures of women walking sideways spelled out:

> Welcome to the Lost Valley of the Witches
> You Are Now Cursed.
> *Don't* Have a Nice Day.

It had been exciting when they arrived, flying behind Ringo on Sam's hastily mended broom into the magically hidden Valley of the Witches. Well, exciting for Sam; Esmelia had sneered that if you'd seen one pointy pile of stones, you'd seen them all. The old witch hadn't stopped moaning ever since. By now, Sam's excitement had definitely worn off. She was glum. Fed up. Cheesed off. She drummed her heels on the rock, and stared at nothing, lost in gloomy glumness.

For three days they had been looking for any clue that might lead them to the spell that created The Black Wand of Ohh Please Don't Turn Me Into Aaaarghh… Ribbett. Sam had shifted heavy rocks, cast spells at cliffs, dug up secret entrances, and crawled into old tombs, and all she'd found had been

bandage-wrapped mummies and a few pots with dried up eyeballs at the bottom. It seemed like she was never going to have a black wand of her own. Plus, she was worried about her grandmother. Lilith Dwale was the only family Sam had and the thought of her being in Diabolica's clutches was horrible.

Suddenly, her thoughts were interrupted by a loud wail from the rocks below. Sam sighed, then shouted, "What is it *now*, Esmelia?"

And that's another thing, Sam grumped to herself. She hadn't been allowed to bring Helza to Egypt. *Oh no. That would mean she might enjoy herself, just a little bit, and the old bag would never allow that.* So Helza had stayed to help Blanche find witches for the new army and she'd been stuck with almost-toothless crabby-face, as usual.

The almost-toothless crabby face of Esmelia popped up from behind another rock. "Stubbed me toe," she moaned. "On a scorpion."

"Oh how awful," snapped Sam. "I hope you didn't hurt it."

Esmelia looked up sharply. "What about *me*, eh? Blinkin' thing stung me and now I got a toe what's swelled up like a loaf of bread. I'll be ages before I can kick anyone with it."

Sam reminded herself she was a *good* witch and just managed to stop herself saying that she would be glad to take over Esmelia's kicking duties, so long as she could practice on Esmelia's own backside. Instead, she asked, "Have you found anything yet?"

"Bah. Scrubbin' about in the dirt and old rocks for three days and what we got to show for it? Blisters, a bunch of dried-up dead people and a toe the size of a pumpkin. I'll never get me boot back on."

However much Esmelia might be annoying her, Sam had to admit that the old witch had a point. It looked like they were wasting their time here and, twice, they had seen broomstick-riding zombie witches flying against the stars. *Maybe,* Sam thought, *she and Esmelia* should *go back and help raise an army*.

With another deep sigh, Sam slipped down off her rock saying, "Let's give it a few more hours before we give up. "If we fly back at night there's a better chance we won't be spotted. And we haven't finished digging here yet."

Sam shouldered a pickaxe and followed a narrow path to where she had blasted a hole in the cliff that morning. She had discovered a small room, though small rooms no longer excited her much. In three days, they had discovered dozens of them and every single one had been like getting a nicely wrapped parcel, only to find it contained socks. There was never anything interesting in them. Just pictures of beetles and the sideways walking women and, if you were lucky, a painted coffin containing a mouldy dead person wrapped in bandages. With a heavy feeling that she was wasting her time, Sam swung her pickaxe at a wall.

To her surprise it went right through. With a little flitter, Ringo flew off her shoulder and through the hole Sam had made. A few seconds later, he came out again and buzzed round her head in excitement.

For the first time in three days, Sam's face lit up in a smile. "Esmelia!" she shouted. "I think I've found something!"

Esmelia limped around the corner with her scorpion-stung toe wrapped in a dirty bandage.

Sam's eyes narrowed. "Where did you get the bandage from?" she asked suspiciously. "We didn't bring any…" And then she remembered where you could find plenty of bandages in the Lost Valley of the Witches, and finished with a gasp "… oh you *didn't*?"

"Well, bandages ain't no good to *them*," snapped Esmelia. "Use as many as you like, bandages ain't going cure nothin' if you've been dead five thousand years."

17 Cobwebs and Deadly Venom in the Dark

The wall crumbled. Behind it was a passageway that led down into darkness and, probably, almost certain death.

"Be careful, Esmelia. These kind of secret passages *always* have deadly booby traps. I've seen it in films," Sam whispered excitedly, laying a warning hand on the old witch's arm. "Poison darts that come shooting out the walls, lakes of fire, huge balls of stone that roll down to flatten you like a gerbil under a steamroller... "

They were close. Sam could feel it. Her heart was playing the xylophone on her ribs and her blood was fizzing. There was big magic down the dark corridor somewhere, and Sam had to stop herself from running towards it. Magic was calling out to her, making her realise how much she *wanted* a wand as powerful as The Black Wand of Ohh Please Don't Turn Me Into Aaaarghh… Ribbett. She needed it like Esmelia needed a bath. With so much power in her hands she could do *anything*. She could swat Diabolica like a mosquito. And Esmelia would no longer be able to hold her back either.

She might even be able to make Lilith give up her secrets...

"Huge balls of stone indeed," said Esmelia sniffed. She took a limping step forward into the gloom. "They makes all that stuff up... waaaahhhHH!"

"Are you alright? Was it a huge ball of stone?" Sam took a careful step forward and held up her wand. "Light," she mumbled. The tip began glowing silver. Esmelia was standing in the corridor with a bucket on her head.

"No. It's a bucket," said Esmelia in a muffled voice.

"Are you hurt?"

"Fat chance of that," sniffed Esmelia. "What sort of booby trap is a bucket on the head, eh? You might as well throw a wet sponge."

Sam walked forward slowly. "Look, the bucket's got a little note on it," she said. In three days Sam had become quite good at reading ancient Egyptian picture writing. "Hmm," she said, "I think it says, 'We're sorry about the bucket, it's supposed to be full of poisonous snakes, but the spider keeps eating them.' Oh."

There was a scuttling noise in the dark. "Oh," repeated Sam.

"Bah, spiders," sneered the old witch. "The thing

about spiders is if you steps on 'em they goes crunch and their insides plop out, ain't it?" She took another step forward, and was instantly swallowed as the ground gave way under her feet.

"Weeeeeek!" squealed Esmelia as she disappeared.

Sam put her head down the hole, "Esmelia?" she shouted, then almost choked. "Gah, it smells like someone's insides have plopped out down there."

"It weren't me, if that's what you're thinkin'" answered Esmelia's faint voice. "And I *knew* that hole was there. In fact, I *meant* to do that."

"Of course you did," Sam shouted back. "So what's down there?"

Esmelia replied slowly as if she were talking to an idiot. "Well, it's difficult to see anything on account of how there's no light and that is tending to make it *very dark*. But somethin's ticklin' the back of me neck."

"It's probably a spider. Don't move until I get there," shouted Sam. Putting her wand between her teeth she climbed carefully into the hole and, bracing her back against the walls with her legs, lowered herself down.

"Pah, I don't think I needs an *apprentice* to protect me from a spider," snapped Esmelia. "I is the *official*

Most Superior High and Wicked Witch you know. I'd like to see the spider what could scare me."

Sam felt solid ground beneath her feet. Cautiously, she raised her wand and it blazed into light. Esmelia was standing in the middle of a cave with her arms crossed and a surly look on her face. She was covered in dust and old cobwebs. Sam didn't take very much notice though. Her attention was being drawn to a spider that was standing behind the old witch. A spider that was roughly the size of a tank. It towered above Esmelia, a great hideous brute with eight eyes flickering cruelly and venom dripping from its fangs. As the light from Sam's wand grew brighter it reared back, its front legs waving about in the smelly air.

Sam's mouth fell open and the blood drained from her face.

"What are you gawpin' at?" snapped Esmelia.

"S-s-s…"

"Spit it out you little maggot."

"There's a spider behind you," Sam gasped.

Esmelia spun round, peering at the dusty floor. "Where? I don't see no spiders, just these great hairy pole things." Slowly she raised her head as her eyes followed the hairy poles up, and up. "Ahh," she said eventually, taking a step back.

"Now would be a good time to step on it," suggested Sam.

Esmelia glanced down at her feet. "I think we're going to need a bigger boot," she replied, backing up a few more inches.

"I'll use a Transformation spell on it," whispered Sam. "It'll just take a second…"

But time had run out. With a terrifying hiss, the spider dropped upon them. Sam smelled its foul breath and glimpsed flashing fangs in the wandlight, then squeezed her eyes closed. A drop of venom fell on her skin, and she closed her eyes tighter. *Any moment now*, she thought, hoping that it would be over quickly…

… Any moment now.

Any moment...

After what felt like three hours, but was probably only two and a half, Sam opened one eye. Inches from her face were several blackly glittering spider eyes, staring straight at her. With a sudden movement, the spider turned to look into Esmelia's face and hissed.

At Sam's side, Esmelia squeaked hysterically, "It's got eight eyes. I got eight fingers. Coincidence? I don't think so."

"Before we die, I just want to say that I almost quite liked you really, underneath it all," Sam squeaked back, trying to stay upright on legs that felt as though they'd much rather not be anywhere near her at the moment.

"Really?" squeaked Esmelia, as squeaking seemed to be the thing to do just then. "I'd like to say the same."

"Thank you."

"Only I can't because I mostly thought you was an annoying little toad."

Then, to the surprise of the two witches, the spider went down on its knees before Sam. They were more surprised when it began rubbing its head against her hand. By the time

THE WHITE WAND

it had rolled onto its back to have its tummy tickled
both witches had gone beyond surprise and had
moved onto flabbergasted amazement with a

large helping of "well, there's something you don't see every day."

Sam slowly reached out and stroked the spider's fur. It was softer than she thought it would be. She tickled it and, while the huge creature wriggled happily under her fingertips, tried to think of something to say while her legs sorted themselves out. Eventually, she came up with "blimey" which seemed to sum everything up nicely.

"Blimey," agreed Esmelia.

Slowly, the terror passed and, once again, Sam felt the irresistible pull of great magic. They were closer now. Her head jerked up. The spider seemed to know what she wanted. It jumped to its feet and bounded away down a dark passage.

"I think it likes us. I think it wants us to follow it," said Sam with awe in her voice.

"Alright, but you go in front. If it decides it's hungry after all, it can eat you while I scarpers."

Sam gave Esmelia a look that would have been withering if Esmelia had been the sort of person who took any notice of withering glances, and set off after her new friend.

18 The Hall of The Witch Queen

The two witches followed the spider through twisting, rocky passageways. Along the way they had to step over several skeletons. There were a few skulls scattered around, too; some still wearing pointy hats. When she wasn't fighting her way through thick cobwebs or panting from the magic that was pulling at her, Sam wondered why the spider was helping them. Every other witch who had found this place had died, horribly. Some were wrapped in thick blankets of web and looked as though they'd had their insides sucked out like a thick milkshake. Sam shuddered and kept her eyes on the giganticly fanged creature ahead of them. The spider was frolicking along like an eager puppy.

At last they came to a great cave. In the center was a shaft in the ground. The spider stopped and peered down into it. Sam threw a stone in and listened for it to hit the bottom. Esmelia took the opportunity to have a rest and perched herself on the lap of a skeleton dressed in rags. While they waited for the stone to drop, she rummaged through the dead witch's pockets. Sam scowled at her.

"*What?*" sneered Esmelia, "It's not like she's going to be wantin'... let's see what have we got here... two bits of string and a mint humbug."

Sam heard a distant clatter as the stone finally hit the floor. "How are we going to get down there?" she asked. "It must be nearly a mile down."

"Well, a broom would've been handy, if a certain brainless little twerp had thought to bring it along."

"I could always use magic," replied Sam thoughtfully. "There's Lady Soo-shi's Floating Leaf spell. We could waft down."

"Whad's it doin' dat fo'?" asked Esmelia through a mouthful of humbug, pointing at the spider. "Ha it god a itch?"

Sam turned to see the giant spider jabbing at his own back with a hairy leg, and said thoughtfully, "Do you think he wants us to get on?"

Esmelia pushed the humbug into her cheek with her tongue. "He can *want* all he likes, I ain't ridin' a spider," she tutted. "It'd be prickly."

"Well, *you* go back for the broom then."

After a short, but furious, argument during which Esmelia accidentally spat the remains of her humbug into Sam's hair, the spider scurried into the hole with the two witches sitting astride its back. Esmelia clutched her apprentice's waist and screamed as air rushed past them. Sam clutched at her hat and grinned. In the darkness below was magic like nothing she'd ever felt before.

Sam wriggled down the spider's backside and lifted her wand. Silvery light glinted off a pile of gold big enough to fill a swimming pool. Esmelia immediately forgot about the horrifying drop through webby darkness. She threw herself into a pile of clinking coins and did the breaststroke through it, screeching, "We're rich, rich... no, forget that: *I'm* rich, rich, RICH!"

Gold. Gold covered columns supported a gold ceiling far above, and gold was inlaid into the picture writing that stretched across every wall.

Sam barely noticed. Her gaze was fixed on a great tomb at the far end of the giant underground room. It was made out of gold, obviously, and in front was a golden alter on which rested the only thing in the room not made of gold: a wooden box.

The magic was stronger here. Sam couldn't fight it any more. She started running. Behind her, Esmelia shrieked, "Oh, the jumble I can buy," and "I'll get a new hat. Yes, *and* a new litter tray for Tiddles."

Sam tore off the box's lid and peered into it. Inside were two scrolls of paper that had been made from the criss-crossed leaves of reeds. With trembling fingers, Sam reached out as if she were putting her hand into a basket of snakes. Taking the first scroll, she pulled her hand out slowly, and gently, gently unrolled it. In the centre was a picture of a wand that Sam had seen before. The Black Wand of Ohh Please Don't Turn Me Into Aaaarghh... Ribbett. The wand in the picture had exactly the same markings, and whoever had painted it had even gone to the trouble of putting in the sparkles. Around the edges of the scroll were what looked like step-by-step instructions.

"What's that then?" snapped a voice behind her.

Sam looked up into the leering face of Esmelia. "It's the spell," she whispered. "We found it." Inside her head, fireworks were going off and an orchestra was playing a song with lots of drums and violins and cannons exploding. With this wand she would be the most powerful witch on Earth and, what was more, it felt *right*. She was *supposed* to have the wand. It was what she was born for. Sam hugged herself and fought down the urge to dance and sing about happy days and what a wonderful world it was.

Stuff was happening inside Esmelia's head, too. Sam had not been the only witch to feel the pull of the spell's great magic and in Sam's shaking fingers was the key to Esmelia becoming Most Superior High and Wicked Witch permanently. The old witch was having trouble stopping herself from rubbing her hands together in glee, so she gave up. Rubbing her hands together in glee, she cackled, "Well, we'd better be off then. People getting worried prob'ly. Nasty world taker-overers to foil. That sort of thing."

"Hang on a second, what's this?" Sam was getting to her feet when something caught her eye. On the side of the great tomb was a picture of a woman. She looked like a witch and had a huge spider standing behind her, but she was carrying a baby. And the baby was a witch too. You could tell because it was wearing a pointed hat and carrying a wand: a black wand.

Bringing her own glowing wand closer, Sam peered at the ancient picture writing. "And lo Queen

Psaman'tah did bring magic into the world," she read. She looked up at Esmelia with excitement. "This is the tomb of the very first witch," she gasped.

"Oh. And that's interestin' is it?" replied Esmelia, inspecting her fingernails and thinking it was time to push some fresh muck underneath them.

Sam ignored her. "This picture says that the queen had a child," she said. "But that's against the oldest law of witchcraft."

Sam crawled around the tomb. She couldn't take her eyes off the pictures as they told their story. "And here it says that she shared the magic with other women, but first they had to agree never to have children. Only her… what's this word… 'daughter' I think… was allowed. And *her* daughter and *her* daughter after her."

Sam stopped, and her face went white in the shadows as she remembered Lilith's words written on the pages of *Think Yourself Witch* back in Pigsnout Wood…

Life isn't fair all the time dearest, but let me tell you this instead. And it's important. The first and highest and most serious of witching laws says that witches aren't allowed to have children. There are horrible punishments for anyone that does.

But for thousands of years…

Then Sam remembered that she had slammed the book closed in a sulk. Under her breath she murmured, "You stupid, stupid twonk."

"Eh? Did you just call me a 'stupid twonk'?"

"No," sighed Sam. "I called *myself* a stupid twonk."

"That's all right then. Quite right too, though I'd have said a stupid useless great cowpat of a twonk."

Sam, the great-great-great-(add a lot of 'greats' here)-granddaughter of the world's first witch and creator of The Black Wand of Ohh Please Don't Turn Me Into Aaaarghh… Ribbett, stood up and put her hand on the tomb of her ancestor. Now she knew why the spider had helped them. It had been Queen Psaman'tah's familiar. It had *recognised* her.

"Yes Esmelia, I think you're probably right," she said. "Stupid useless great cowpat of a twonk is just about right."

"Well, I'm glad we got that sorted out. Now, let's get out of here. Where's that blinkin' spider?"

As Esmelia shuffled off on her bandaged foot, Sam stood dazed and confused and – if she was honest – more than a little bit pleased that she might have a famous queen for a great-great-great-etc-etc-grandmother. She followed Esmelia as if she were in a dream, then stopped, pulled herself together, and turned back. There was a second scroll in the box and she had nearly forgotten. Quickly, she pushed it into her vest where Ringo could look after it and ran.

19 Unravelling the Scroll of the Black Wand

Sam and Helza were sat on a log in the forest near Sawyer Bottom, having the same conversation that so many young girls of their age do.

"So, you think you're the great-great-great-and-so-on-granddaughter of a 5,000-year-old Egyptian Queen who first brought magic into the world and kept a gigantic spider as a pet?" said Helza. "Wowzers. Does that make you a princess?" She stopped and looked Sam up and down. "You don't *look* like a princess. Princesses don't have twigs in their hair. There's a test though, we could use it if you like? Something with peas and beds. Do you ever pe…"

"I'm *not* a princess and if you're not going to take me seriously then I won't bother talking to you," Sam snapped at her friend.

"OK OK, don't blow your lid. So, you *think* you might be related to this Ancient Egyptian fruit loop, huh? But all you *really* know is that dear old granny was a witch who, like, broke the first rule of witchcraft and that."

"It's more than that," replied Sam. "I'm *sure* that Lilith was about to tell me that for thousands of years one family of witches have been secretly having children. Besides, I can just *feel* it, and I think it might be why I'm, you know, good at magic. I think it may go from mother to daughter." She blushed.

"So that would mean your mom is a witch, too?"

"Yes, but Lilith won't tell me who she is."

"Oh *no*! You know what that means, don't you?"

Sam panicked at the look of horror in Helza's eyes. "What?" she gulped.

"It means… your mother is probably… *Esmelia*!" Helza started giggling. "Hey, I wouldn't want to be the one to break *that* news to you either."

Between clenched teeth, Sam said, "This is serious. It could be important!"

"Hey chillax," said Helza, putting an arm around her friend's shoulders. "I'm only kidding. When all this is over we'll get Cakula to release you from your apprenticeship and I'll totally help you find your mom. Until then, I'd keep quiet about it if I were you. If the mouldy old bags round here knew you might be a witch

child they'd flip their wigs... And talking of mouldy old bags, check out this old biddy. I mean, oh – *my – gosh*."

Sam's eyes followed Helza's pointing finger to see a bent old witch wheezing towards them with a walking stick in each hand and all the speed and liveliness of a bun. In the time it took for her to reach them, Helza and Sam could have taken a course of pottery lessons. Finally, she arrived at their log. Up close, the old witch's face was moving like she was trying to eat her own mouth from the inside. She squinted at them and cackled, "Which way's the penguins?"

Helza pointed off into the woods. "Keep going that way and you'll find them eventually."

"Ooo, thank you young man." The elderly woman began shuffling away in the opposite direction to the one Helza had pointed in, then stopped and pulled a withered apple out of her pocket. "WOULD YOU LIKE A BITE OF THIS ROSY APPLE, DEARIE?" she screamed at the top of her lungs, even though she had moved less than six inches.

Helza screwed her face up. "Errr... No. Not really."

"That was a bit mean of you. She might get lost," Sam tutted when the witch had managed to get more than ten feet away.

"You think? Well, she *asked* which way to the penguins. I just pointed her towards the North Pole." Helza shrugged. "Besides, the old bags never seem to get lost. Put some food out for them and they all flock back like homing pigeons."

Sam and Helza watched as the witch remembered that she was carrying something, looked at the apple with a cry of surprise, and bit into it. A second later she keeled over into a pile of dead leaves and started snoring.

"So that's our army, is it?" Sam asked.

"Yup," replied Helza. "Thirty-eight witches are all we found. None of them under a hundred years old and they're all kind of, y'know. Wooooo, wooooo..." Helza whirled her finger around at the side of her head. "*Bonkers*; that's the word I'm looking for," she finished.

"Let's hope we can figure out how to make this wand then," Sam said. "Should we go back and see how they're getting on?"

"I guess so," said Helza, standing and giving Sam a hand up. "But if they're *still* arguing with the ghosts, I *will* have to poison someone."

The two girls walked slowly back towards Blanche Nighly's small house in the gathering gloom. As they got closer, they saw more elderly witches hobbling around in the twilight. One was head-butting a tree. Another was sitting in an old-fashioned wicker wheelchair with a slice of bread on her head. Sam waved and shouted, "Hello Nanna Wonk!"

"Meeep," squealed Nanna Wonk, as she died for the third time that week.

Soft candlelight spilled from Blanche's tumbledown cottage. As they approached, Sam and Helza heard the deep voices of long-dead professors. It had been agreed that a spell of such power needed proper translation. After all, if the slightest thing went wrong, it was quite possible that Sam could turn the whole planet into a small pot plant called Debbie. So Blanche had contacted ghosts who were experts in Ancient Egyptian to help decipher the Scroll of The Black Wand. Unfortunately, none of the professors could agree with each other. They had been shouting for nearly a week and the witches were no closer to knowing exactly how the magic should be done.

"That's not the chicken-headed goddess B'kurk,"

yelled a voice hotly. "It's a speck of fly poo. Any fool can see that! Which means that the ritual must be performed with a bunch of fresh spinach."

"I'm sorry, but Professor Ringworm is out of his tiny excuse for a mind," barked another. "That is *obviously* the ancient symbol of Brrrr Chiliout Ayntit and means that the magical ceremony must be attended by dancing witches dressed as nature provides."

There was a pause, then a familiar voice screeched, "Does he mean in the nudie? He does, doesn't he? That's disgustin'. I ain't doin' it."

A voice that Sam had come to recognise cut in. It belonged to Wisteria Wickham, Helza's new boss. She said, "Oh no, you've got it all wrong Esmelia. Dancing for the universe dressed only in the moonlight is beautifully cosmic. You'll love it. It feels like the power of the earth is flowing into you."

"You'll feel the power of my finger flowing into you in a minute."

Helza looked at Sam, and rolled her eyes. "Doesn't sound like they've worked it out yet," she said.

Sam shook her head. "And no Lilith yet, either. I'm getting really worried about her."

20 *A World of Darkness*

"Where *is* she?" screamed Diabolica. A thousand shuffling zombie witches took a shuffling step backwards in the face of her fury.

"I *told* you to bring me Sam, and what do I get?" The power-crazed sorceress kicked at a pile with one of her toweringly high-heeled shoes. "Three hundred sets of false teeth! For the very last time, *what* are you supposed to find for your glorious queen?"

The zombie witches gaped at one another and scratched their heads. Eventually, one shuffled forward and groaned, "Err... Teeef. Pretty Teef. Di-ab-ol-ic-ca."

Power crackled from The Black Wand of Ohh Please Don't Turn Me Into Aaaarghh... Ribbett. "Ribb-ett," droned a zombie-witch-frog, before shuffling off to join several others in a corner.

Diabolica flicked the wand again. In a large mirror by the throne, an image of Sam appeared. Diabolica counted to ten, took a breath, and pointed to it. Nine hundred and ninety-nine pairs of eyes followed. "For the last time you moronic bunch of dolts, idiots and cheese-headed cretins, *this* is what I want," she shouted. "Not false teeth. *This*! A girl. A human *girl*. Her name is Sam. I want every one of you in the air. Search everywhere. Use magic. Just find her for me. *NOW*!"

The army of zombie witches stood gaping at her. Red faced, Diabolica screeched, "Fly my uglies, fly."

Brooms filled the sky around the Bleak Fortress like a cloud of mosquitoes and Diabolica sank into the Great Throne of the Most Superior High and Wicked Witch with a curse on her perfect lips. There was a wet squelch and she stood again quickly. A flat frog was spread all over the seat. "Another dress ruined," spat Diabolica, wiping away the squishy remains. "I have had it up to *here* with frogs."

She sat and, without thinking, picked up *Think Yourself Witch*. Now, at last, the writing began to change. Diabolica's eye's widened. She held her breath and watched as lines wriggled and shuffled across the page, until they spelled…

Bwah ha ha HA HA HA HA HA!

"Shut up," snarled Diabolica. But Lilith had decided that the time had come to talk. Diabolica's eyes flicked over the page as new words appeared.

Have you got what it takes to take over the world?

Answer these questions and find out.

1. *As a power-crazed, evil sorceress your greatest achievement is…*

a. *Creating an army of zombie witches who couldn't find their own bottoms with a map and a DetectoBum bottom detector.*

b. *Hoarding the biggest treasure trove of false teeth the world has ever seen, thus going down in history as Susan the Denture Queen.*

c. *Becoming the proud owner of a frog sanctuary.*

d. *Being outwitted, foiled and outwitted again by your own long-lost daughter and, best of all… wait for it… Esmelia Sniff!*

To finish, Lilith added, *Bwah ha ha HA HA HA HA HA!* again, just to make sure it hadn't slipped past Diabolica the first time.

"Laugh all you like Lilith Dwale, but I *will* find Sam," sneered Diabolica. "There are better servants coming than those shuffling fools. Can you feel what I'm doing to the magic? I *know* you can. It is darkening, and you know what that means, don't you?"

You're bringing them back?

Diabolica curled her lip and her finger jabbed at the page. "Yes, they're *all* coming back. Coming to serve *me*. The wraiths, the ghouls, the banshees, the werewolves, the ghastly things with too many heads. All of them. And then I will set loose such magics as the world has never seen... Plus, I'm also toying with the idea of making all the guinea pigs explode. Don't ask me why, it just seems like fun."

She paused and looked at the book in her lap. Nothing happened. "This is the bit where you tell me I'm mad and it will never work," she prompted.

You're mad. It will never work.

"Booooring," Diabolica declared. "I'll show you how it works. Watch."

Diabolica laid the book, open, on a small table. She stood, and held The Black Wand of Ohh Please Don't Turn Me Into Aaaarghh... Ribbett before her. Her lips moved and a shimmering globe appeared in the dim cavern of the Bleak Fortress's Throne Room. A globe more perfect than anything you'd find in a geography classroom. Tiny chains of mountains marched across continents, cities were made up of minuscule buildings and ships almost too small to see sailed the heaving oceans. Shining faintly over everything were twisting threads of light, some as thick as ribbons, others so fine they could barely be seen.

"Magic," breathed Diabolica, tracing one of the threads with the tip of The Black Wand of Ohh Please Don't Turn Me Into Aaaarghh… Ribbett. "It's in everything and connects everything. But, of course, you knew that already." She glanced at *Think Yourself Witch*.

Don't do it, Diabolica. This magic is too dark, even for you. It will change you. It will change everything…

"That is the plan," jeered the power-crazed sorceress. "You've spent too long with your head in a book, that's your trouble. No imagination. No idea of what's *possible*."

The writing changed again. This time Lilith wrote:
Please Diabolica. It's not too late, You have a daughter, what about her?

Diabolica curled her lip again, and turned back to

the globe. Threads of magic twined around the Earth in every colour of the rainbow, but here and there were tiny points of jet black that throbbed with evil. With the tip of her wand, Diabolica touched one. "And here's the Bleak Fortress," she whispered.

Closing her eyes, Diabolica summoned all the magic that a powerful sorceress can command and combined it with the awesome power of the The Black Wand of Ohh Please Don't Turn Me Into Aaaarghh… Ribbett. Around her a huge swirl of black power began to spin. With a gasp, Diabolica channelled it through The Black Wand of Ohh Please Don't Turn Me Into Aaaarghh… Ribbett and into the tiny point of black light that was the Bleak Fortress.

The skies above Transylvania darkened and somewhere on the very edge of sound, there was a horrible whispering, rustling noise and a low, evil growl. On Diabolica's globe the black dot pulsed harder and began to grow. Every other spark of blackness throbbed in time with it, and slowly, slowly, seeped evil into the web of magic that covered the Earth. For an instant, the whole world spun in blackness. Diabolica's eyes snapped open and she staggered back away from the globe.

"*Yes,*" she panted, "They're coming. I can feel them. All the wild things are coming back. They can feel the world getting darker. It's almost ready for them."

Slowly, her breathing returned to normal. Diabolica inspected the fading globe. The black points were bigger now and among the bright ribbons were threads of utter darkness. "Oh," she smiled. "I love doing that."

On the table *Think Yourself Witch* riffled its pages in horror.

Uh oh, wrote Lilith.

21 Digging Up Dreadful

As if she were poking at a sore tooth with her tongue, Sam called up a tiny dribble of magic and winced. There was a tang of evil to it that made her feel grubby. With a shiver, she let it fizz away into the air and turned her attention back to finding the path between the trees.

"I still don't like this," she said, for the thirteenth time. "I didn't become a witch so I could dig up dead people."

Bah, what twaddle you does talk," Esmelia huffed in reply. "A sock puppet'd make a betterer witch than you. Diggin' up graves by moonlight is what your basic witchin' is all about," she paused, then added, "Very useful, your skellingtons. All sorts of stuff you can make with 'em …"

"It's horrible," snapped Sam. "The dead should be allowed to rest in peace."

"Rubbish," replied Esmelia. "If *you* was dead, what would you like better? Bein' stuck inside a stuffy coffin for ever, or bein' made into an eye-catchin' pair of salad tongs and matching napkin rings?"

With an oddly thick mist clinging to their ankles

like gloopy porridge, Sam, Helza, and Esmelia, traipsed through the midnight woods. At last the Scroll of the Black Wand had been translated, and while Blanche, Wisteria and the small army made sure that everything was ready for the spell back at Sawyer Bottom, the three of them had been sent out on a special mission. Sam shivered, and not just because of the grisly job ahead. Between the frosty branches above stars twinkled as usual but there was a feeling of gloom in the air, as if something was waiting, sharpening its claws, and getting ready to pounce. Every now and again, the figures of broomstick riding zombie-witches could be seen against the crescent moon, criss-crossing the skies.

Feeling rather sick at the thought of the unusual white salad tongs she'd used so many times back in Esmelia's cottage, Sam looked to Helza for help.

Helza was busily collecting fungi from the trees they passed, muttering things like "Sickly Gimprash, yes you'll do for a Potion of Neverending Despair," and "Wow, Pixie's Shinybuttock, that's rare…" She caught Sam's look and interrupted herself, "…What?"

"I was just saying to Esmelia that digging up dead people and stealing their bones is wrong."

Helza shrugged and stuffed a handful of Pixie's

Shinybuttock into her rucksack. "Whatevs. The scroll says the new wand needs to be made with the bone of a witch. Where else are we going to get one?"

"We could have picked a bone up in Egypt, they were just laying around over there," Sam grumbled.

"Yeah, but Diabiolica's zombie things are everywhere now and there's *loads* of dead witches around here. This place used to be crawling with them in the old days." Helza stopped. "Hey, we're here."

Ahead of them was a crumbling wall with a tall iron gate that was covered in ivy and hanging off its hinges. On the other side, Sam could see the shapes of gravestones and statues looming among the trees in the fog. She gritted her teeth and hissed, "Come on then. Let's get it over with."

Behind her, Esmelia chuckled a chuckle that might easily have been mistaken for a cackle. Soon, she would have her gnarly old hands on a wand as powerful as The Black Wand of Ohh Please Don't Turn Me Into Aaaarghh... Ribbett. She patted her apprentice on the shoulder and crooned, "Don't you worry dearie. It's just like diggin' up potatoes. Only more fun. And sometimes you find they was buried in good quality clothes, too. It's even better'n a jumble sale is that."

Helza shooed a cawing raven off a gravestone and scraped moss from the carved letters. The three witches squinted at the rough writing.

PENNY DREADFUL
1633(ish) – 1756
She was a witch, so we hanged her

By the light of the silvery moon, they nodded to each other and began to dig...

Two hours of digging later, Esmelia's and Sam's spades banged into the wood of a coffin lid with two dull knocks.

"Come in," giggled Helza. Sam glared at her.

The witches heaved the coffin up and prised open the lid. Resting inside was the skeleton of Penny Dreadful, wearing an old fashioned black dress and a shawl around her neck. On her chest was an envelope. In flowing letters on the front was the word, "Sam." Which was a surprise. And even though she'd had a few of those recently, this one made goosebumps prickle along Sam's arms. Among the things that she had least expected to find in Penny Dreadful's centuries-old coffin were a pine-fresh smell and a letter addressed to herself. Her nose twitched. She'd been right about the smell at least.

White faced, Sam took the envelope and gingerly opened it. With shaking hands, she pulled a piece of paper from the envelope. Taking her first breath for nearly a minute and a half, she read:

Dug me up for me bones have ye? Thass nice. I allus says it does a body good to get sum fresh air. Mind though, at my age, I has the aches in most of me old bones, but me left arm bone is prob'ly sound. I'd use that'n if I was ye. A werd in yer ear, farm one witch to another. When I wus alive I seed the futcher an' I knows all about ye I does young Sam.

The fate o' the werld be in yer hands, an ye be all what stands 'agin the Deadly Nightshade. It be up to ye, but afore ye goes changin' the futcher ye think careful now. If'n ye wanted it, ye'd be Queen o' the Werld, an a witch queen might'n not be so bad, eh? Jest arsk that saucy Esmelia Sniff varmint. She... well now. I could tells ye all about Esmelia I s'poses, but where'd be the larf in that? I does like a larf.

Since I is talkin' about havin' a larf, I sees Esmelia be a thief whom be out t'steal me clothes. They won't be fittin' her anyhows, but tells the ole biddie t' take me shawl. I put some powder in it what I made speshal out of the Pizen Ivy. It'll gives her the itches somethin' terruble, so it will.

Ye thinks about what I tole ye Sam. Ye got the power, it be up t'ye how ye uses it.

May the night protect ye

P. Dreadful

"What's it say?" demanded Esmelia. "It's a curse ain't it? Just my luck to dig up one of them mean ones."

Sam shook her head. Looking up in wonder, she whispered, "She knew we were coming. She... errr... she thought her left arm would make a good wand." For some reason, Sam found she didn't want to tell what she had read. She screwed the note up and thrust it into her pocket.

Esmelia looked down at the remains of Penny Dreadful and moaned, "Tut, would you look at that, she was a stumpy one, weren't she? Almost a blinkin' dwarf. I'll never get into that dress."

"Yes, but the shawl will be alright," Sam replied absently. Leaning over, she took the longest bone from Penny Dreadful's left arm and gently wrapped it in a piece of cloth.

When the coffin had been placed back in the ground and reburied, Esmelia pulled her new shawl around her neck and the three witches turned to go. Sam passed the bone to Esmelia. "Here," she said. "You'll need to carve this into the new black wand."

The small group turned away and began the hike back to Sawyer Bottom through the mist. Half a mile down the narrow path, Esmelia let the cloth drop off from the bone and began scratching her back with it. Behind them, a dark figure shuffled out from behind a statue of a weeping angel. "Saaam," it groaned. "New. Black. Wand… Teef."

22 The Whittling

Something howled in the forest. Esmelia Sniff, wicked witch, screamed "wah" and fell backwards off the tree stump she was perched upon. Howling, she could cope with. Wolves, monkeys, even howling donkeys held no terror for Esmelia Sniff. Throwing old boots usually shut most howlers up. But she was almost certain that this howl wasn't being howled by anything natural. It was wolf*ish*, but wolves didn't usually sound quite so *hungry*. Or, if Esmelia was honest with herself, quite so scary. Whatever was howling out in the woods sounded as though it would snap a thrown boot out of the air, rip it to shreds and spit it back at her.

And, as if the howling wasn't bad enough, Esmelia was itching all over. She was the kind of person who was always scratching her armpits and, occasionally, when no one was looking, other parts as well, but this was much worse than her usual itches. And no matter how much she scratched it wouldn't stop. "Fleas," she muttered to herself, clawing at the back of her neck. "Nothin' wrong with havin' fleas. I always *wanted* to get the fleas."

While Esmelia lay on her back scratching furiously, two ancient witches shambled past with enormous bundles of wood on their backs.

"Oooo Enid, look at that young man," crowed one, pointing at Esmelia with her walking stick. "He's havin' a fit."

"What's that you say," screeched Enid, cupping her ear with a hand. "A fit? Out here in the woods? The dirty little beggar."

Scowling, Esmelia settled herself back on the log and carried on whittling mystic symbols and magical runes into Penny Dreadful's arm bone. It was already looking less boney and more wandy and Esmelia could feel the beginnings of a powerful magical fizz within it. Surprisingly, the old witch was making a beautiful job of the carving. Esmelia wasn't good at much, apart from causing painful injuries armed only with a finger, but she was an expert with a knife. Before Sam had arrived at her cottage, she had spent years and years alone at night without a TV and had needed her hobbies to stop her from going completely mad. It hadn't worked, of course; she *had* gone completely mad, but she had also become a wonderful whittler.

Every so often Esmelia stopped to scratch and

glance at the picture of The Black Wand of Ohh Please Don't Turn Me Into Aaaarghh… Ribbett on the scroll. All the while she murmured to herself. Someone with excellent hearing might have heard her saying things like… "Remind the mouldy little cabbage who's boss round here" or "cheeky maggot, and me the *official* Most Superior High and Wicked Witch and all," or "Gold. Lots and lots of luvverly gold there was." After a few minutes Tiddles trotted out of the forest with an endangered species hanging from his mouth and curled up at her feet. Esmelia rubbed her cat behind the ears, which made Tiddle miaow in confusion. Esmelia *never* rubbed his ears.

"Nearly finished Tiddles," Esmelia cackled. "And once the little twerp has magicked the wand, we'll be goin' up in the world, eh? I'll be proper, not-acting Most Superior High and Wicked Witch, and you'll be… err… Most Superior High and Wicked Cat, or something."

Tiddles looked at her with unblinking yellow eyes. He *already* thought of himself as Most Superior High and Wicked Cat. Every cat does.

"Of course, *she'll* reckon we betrayed her and get in a right old tizz about it," Esmelia continued. "Which'll mean the little chump will moan on and on and on and on. But I'll tell her to go boil her head, shan't I? She's *my* apprentice and I was *supposed* to be Most Superior High and Wicked Witch. It's only puttin' all her tinkerin' and meddlin' right."

Esmelia stared into Tiddles' eyes. "And you can stop lookin' at me like that," she muttered. "I'm a wicked witch I am. It's me *job* to go around betraying people and pinchin' stuff."

Tiddles continued to stare at her.

"Bah, I said stop it you pesky

moggie. Beatin' that ninny Danglybobica will be easy. I got tricks I have. *And* she burned me house down. And me jumble! What sort of wicked witch would I be if I didn't poke her to a jelly, eh?"

Tiddles shook his head and slunk off back into the forest. If he worked hard and put in the effort, he was sure that the endangered species could soon become an extinct species.

"And don't think I don't know it was you sleepin' on me face all the time what gave me the fleas," Esmelia shouted after him. She harrumphed, then returned to her whittling and went over her plan again. It was a good plan; one of her best. The sort of sneaky devious plan that any witch could be proud of. If witches gave out awards for dastardly plans, this one would easily win her a basket of toads.

Strangely though, the closer she got to actually carrying out the plan, the less happy Esmelia was about it. The old witch gritted her two teeth together. *It must be the fleas*, she decided. The itching was driving her completely barmy.

23 Dance of the Crones

Sam carried the carved arm bone of Penny Dreadful into the circle of witches. She was trembling with excitement and Penny Dreadful's words were spinning around her head; "Ye got the power, it be up t'ye how ye uses it." She was going to make a wand to rival The Black Wand of Ohh Please Don't Turn Me Into Aaaarghh… Ribbett. With such power in her hands she would become the greatest witch in the world. Possibly even the greatest witch ever. Of course, she reminded herself, she definitely, absolutely, certainly didn't want to become a witch *queen*. That would just make her as bad as Diabolica. Sam had already decided that she would use the power to put everything back the way it was supposed to be, but after that… Well, she could do anything she pleased, couldn't she? Cakula would be so grateful that she would release her from her apprenticeship to Esmelia and then maybe she and Helza could go away somewhere and invent new spells and potions…

As she passed Esmelia, Sam winked and whispered, "Well done. You did a brilliant job." Noticing that

Esmelia was absent-mindedly scratching herself, Sam couldn't hold back a smile. It wasn't really *nasty,* she told herself. Itching powder was the sort of joke that anyone her age might play and it hadn't been her idea anyway.

"Bah," grumped Esmelia, Inside though, she felt a tiny flicker of pride. And, when she thought of what she was about to do, something else that she'd never felt before. It was a sort of dull grey miserable feeling in the pit of her stomach. "Must be trapped wind," she muttered to herself then shoved a hand down the back of her dress and clawed at her skin. The fleas were on fire tonight.

Slowly, while every witch watched in silence, Sam mounted a small stage that had been set up in the middle of a clearing. Behind it a huge bonfire spat flames at the sky. Helza was already there, stirring a cauldron with an intense look of concentration on her face. She was wearing shorts and a vest.

Sam took her place behind the cauldron. "What's the bonfire for?" She whispered Helza. "There wasn't a bonfire in the scroll."

Helza looked up from the bubbling brew she was making, and whispered back, "The ghost professors said it wouldn't make any difference and the old ones wanted to toast marshmallows later. Plus we thought it might help keep them warm. Look at the poor old dears."

Sam looked out into the clearing, where a ring of shivering old women stood ready. Some were wearing old-fashioned stripy swimming costumes that came down below their knees, others wore vests and knickers or the kind of enormous and highly complicated underwear that old women seem to love. Even Esmelia had hitched her skirt up far enough that you could just make out a tiny white stripe of shin between the top of her boots and the hem. Only Wisteria Wickham was completely naked. Sam winced and looked away as Wisteria did a pirouette.

"*Why?*" Sam mouthed at Helza.

"Apparently they don't have to dance, like, *totally* naked, so long as they're showing some skin," Helza replied, then shrugged, "Wisteria just likes it. I told you it's gross."

"You weren't kidding…" began Sam. Helza flapped a hand to shush her, and threw the last ingredient into the cauldron. A vast thunderclap filled the air. Sam felt the earth beneath her feet begin to shake. Helza backed away, and nodded at her friend. "It's ready," she shouted. "You go girl."

Helza scampered away to join the ring of witches. Sam realized her hair was standing on end, which was quite an achievement considering how long it had been since she had washed it. She gulped. This was it. She was either going to make herself the most powerful witch ever or, if anything went wrong, make a very very big mess.

Sam raised the wand above her head. The ground shuddered again, and the ring of witches joined hands. "TONIGHT WE PERFORM THE GREATEST MAGIC!" she shouted at the top of her voice. "TONIGHT WE CONJURE WITH THE UNIVERSE!"

"Eh?" Called one of the elderly witches. "She's going to conjure a unicycle? That don't sound very impressive. Is she going to pull some flowers out her sleeve after?"

"Shh, Enid," shouted the witch next to her. "She said uni*verse*."

"Oh, uni*verse*. That's different that is. Get on with it then young lady."

"TONIGHT, THE STARS THEMSELVES ARE OURS TO COMMAND."

She paused, and yelled, "BEGIN!"

Forty-two cracking voices were raised in an ancient droning chant. With creaky movements, the witches began the ancient dance set out in the Scroll of the Black Wand. First was the symbolic dipping of the toe into the seas of magic.

"You puts your left leg in."

Sam plunged the carved bone wand into Helza's brew. Sheets of lightning flickered across the sky and the ground heaved below her feet.

"You pulls your left leg out," chanted the witches, taking their left legs out of the circle.

In the cauldron, strange lights flickered in colours Sam had never seen before. The liquid bubbled furiously.

"In out in out and shakes it all about."

"EARTH!" called Sam. The ground shuddered and groaned beneath her feet and shook all about in response to the spell. Magic was dragged from mud and clay and rock and stone and poured into the boiling cauldron, which began belching hot liquid like a volcano.

The witches made a mystical gesture with their hands and twirled on the spot. "You does the hocus pocus and you turns about," they droned. From the corner of her eye, Sam saw Esmelia was clawing at herself and, for a second, her grin returned.

There was no time to watch. "AIR!" she screamed. At once, the wind whipped into a howling tornado, a twirling whirlwind that was centred on the cauldron. It was, indeed, turning about.

The ring of witches rushed towards the stage as fast as a ring of creaky old ladies can, their arms in the air. "Oooooooh the hocus pocus," they shouted. Then hobbled back to their original positions. Esmelia, meanwhile, was jumping about on the spot, her arms and legs going in several directions, and her hands trying to grab hold of every part of her body at once.

THE WHITE WAND

"Yeah, Esmelia. That's it. You're getting it now," called Wisteria Wickham. "Dance, you crazy lady. Dance!"

Around the circle, witches struggled to stay on their feet. "Knees bent," the chanted. "Hands raised." Their voices were carried away on the gale. And now came the call to the old Egyptian Sun God: "Ra, Ra, Ra!"

Sam gripped the side of the cauldron and stared into it. Helza's potion had vanished, but at the bottom the carved wand had been transformed. It was black.

Magic glittered up and down its length. Greedily, Sam snatched it up. It was her turn now.

Out in the circle, Esmelia could bear it no longer. "Aaaaargh," she moaned into the whipping wind. "Flippin' fleas are drivin' me nuts." With her legs jerking in all directions she began clawing at the buttons on her dress.

"Groovy, Esmelia. Who needs clothes, right?" shouted Wisteria. "Feel the power flowing through you."

Sam lifted the wand high, and spared a glance for Ringo who was weaving his front legs as he summoned magic for her. Sam smiled at him. A smile that turned into a laugh of sheer delight at she felt the magic rise. Her own power surged into the wand and joined with it. She could feel a breathtaking, giddying amount of magic in the wand. But not enough, Sam thought. Not nearly enough.

"AND *EVERY*THING!" She shrieked. Lightning crashed from the sky into the tip of the wand. "Not *enough*!" groaned Sam as huge energies whirled through her. She reached out with her magic, higher and higher, into the very stars themselves. Great blooms of light appeared across the sky as one by one, distant suns gave up their power to the wand and exploded. Sam rose in the air, twisting this way and that as the power flowed through her. She felt like she was going to tear apart with it. "Hold on Ringo," she shouted, and reached even higher. Black holes at the very edge of the universe collapsed at her command and their power flooded through her into the wand.

It was enough.

Enough.

But Sam couldn't stop it. She opened her mouth to scream. She had gone too far, and now the wand would take her too…

Ringo's pincers clicked, once. As if snipping a thread. It stopped. Sam fell to the ground like a dropped trifle.

"And *that's* what it's all about," chanted the ring of witches.

24 The White Wand

"Sam, *Sam*! Are you alright?" A distant voice was calling to her. Sam decided to ignore it and float away. She felt a sharp sting as someone slapped her face.

"Ouch! Helza that *really* hurt." Sam opened her eyes and pushed herself to her knees. Forty-two pairs of eyes squinted down into her lap where her hand was still clenched around the wand. A voice at the back said, "Is it *supposed* to look like that, dearie?"

She looked down. In her hand was a wand. It was a wand of incredible power. You could tell because it was glinting with little tings of magic. But it wasn't black. It was pure white. For a moment she stared, twisting it this way and that, wondering what had gone wrong. The wand seemed perfect though, and it wanted a Name. This was an important moment. Sam could feel it. The wand demanded to be given the Name it would carry forever.

"Ladies and… errr… other ladies," she called. "The White Wand of…" she swept it upwards so everyone could see. And nearly jabbed Esmelia in the face.

"… Oi you could have someone's eye out with that," the old witch squealed.

For a second the universe stopped. The wand had been Named. It was The White Wand of… Oi You Could Have Someone's Eye Out With That.

The universe started again. It was a bit disappointed really.

Sam's head snapped around. Esmelia was standing behind her in an old vest stained with sweat and scraps of old egg. A false beard was tucked down the front, making it look like she had a hairy chest. She was also wearing what Sam could only think of as 'undergarments.' They were long and ended with frilly lace at her knees. And there were slugs and a hole. Sam decided it was better not to look at the hole. Her eyes met Esmelia's and the old witch held out a gnarly old hand.

"I'll have that, if you please," she leered, scratching an armpit.

"W-What?" Sam stared at Esmelia as if she was mad, which, of course, she was.

"Witchin' law number 2,346, section 3, clause b," said Esmelia triumphantly. "Remember? You is still my apprentice. So, you does what I tells you. Plus, accordin' to *The Cackler*, I'm *officially* actin' Most Superior High and Wicked Witch what with old Croakula bein' all frogginated."

"B-But I *made* it," gasped Sam in shock. She clutched The White Wand of… Oi You Could Have Someone's Eye Out With That to her chest and added, "It's mine."

"Wrong. Property of the Most Superior High and Wicked Witch, that is. And as there ain't no other Most Superior High and Wicked Witch available, I'm her. So hand it over you little maggot."

"Cakula!" gasped Sam. "Of course. *She'll* sort this out. Where is she?"

"Waaaay ahead of you," called Helza. She was running from Blanche's house with the frog held in her cupped hands. "Got her right here."

"Oh, silly old Esmelia," cackled Esmelia. "The batty old bint forgot all about froggy. Ooops. Off you goes then. De-frog the vampire."

Sam breathed a sigh of relief and stood, covered in mud and shivering from cold and exhaustion. She lifted The White Wand of… Oi You Could Have Someone's Eye Out With That and closed her eyes. With a whispered word, she let the magic flow, guiding it to

break the spell on Cakula and restore the vampire witch to herself.

The magic flowed around the frog in gentle white ribbons. The little creature glowed in the darkness. Then…

… "Ribbett."

"Oh deary deary me," cackled Esmelia. And stopped. She had been looking forward to the look on Sam's face when she realised that the frog wasn't going to turn into a Most Superior High and Wicked Witch, but now she saw it she found didn't like it at all. In fact, Sam's look of sheer misery seemed to be catching.

Sam, meanwhile, stared at the frog. The wand was at least as powerful as The Black Wand of Ohh Please Don't Turn Me Into Aaaarghh… Ribbett. She knew it was. And yet it hadn't broken the spell. Then she understood.

"That's not Cakula," she whispered. "You swapped frogs. You vicious mean, traitorous old hag."

Esmelia scowled, and snatched the wand out of Sam's limp hand. "Well, you'd know all about betrayin' people, wouldn't you" She sneered. "I told you I was *supposed* to be Most Superior High and Wicked Witch, and I told you I had a few tricks up me vest. You never listens, that's your problem."

Helza stepped forward. "Hey, give her that back. It's *hers*. She's the one who figured out how to make it, and you're sooo *not* the Most Superior High and Wicked Witch. If anyone is right now, it's Diabolica."

Esmelia raised her new wand and peered at it. She had to admit the little toad had done a lovely job on it. Except the colour of course. White was strictly for the kind of witches that floated around tinkling and saying things like "You *will* go to the ball."

"Ha, why don't we just give it to *her*, then?" Esmelia cackled.

"Yes, why *don't* you just give it to me?" called a chocolaty voice from the woods. "It would save *such* a lot of fuss and bother."

Forty-three witches spun around, some more quickly than others. Diabolica stepped out from the darkness between the trees. She was a vision of loveliness in shimmering white. In one hand she held The Black Wand of Ohh Please Don't Turn Me Into Aaaarghh… Ribbett and at her back was an army of drooling witches.

"Thank you *so* much for the bonfire and that *wonderful* magical display," continued Diabolica. "We were having a little trouble finding you until then."

Still no one else spoke, except Esmelia who muttered "drat". She had been planning to surprise Diabolica at the Bleak Fortress after she'd had time to practice with the wand and, most importantly, when she had some clothes on.

Diabolica took another couple of steps forward, and spotted her daughter. "Why Samantha darling, you look *dreadful*," she smiled. "But don't worry, mummy's here to make it all better." Then, she raised The Black Wand of Ohh Please Don't Turn Me Into Aaaarghh… Ribbett and shouted now, "Now!"

25 The Battle of Sawyer Bottom

The zombie witches shuffled forward. Through tired eyes, Sam saw the hated face of Diabolica, smiling in the red glow of firelight. In her tired mind, she heard the words, "mummy's here" over and over again. She shook herself. It didn't mean anything. It was just more proof that Diabolica Nightshade was mad as weasels.

Sam slipped the old wooden wand Esmelia had made for her months before from her back pocket. Around her, old witches began to cackle and rub their hands together in glee.

"Ooo Enid," crowed one. "I think these youngsters are looking for a spot of bother."

"What's that you say?" A fight is it? I haven't had a good scrap since me hip replacement. I used to be quite tasty in the old days, you know."

A paper bag filled with extra-hard toffees flew out of the huddle and caught one of the zombie witches on the forehead. She keeled over like a sack of eels.

"Ha, weren't expecting that, was she?"

The battle began very very slowly. One side shuffled, glassy-eyed and gaping, with a war cry of "Di-a-bol-i-ca." The other advanced, wheezing, to meet the enemy with mutters of "teach these young zombie whippersnappers a thing or two."

A walking stick lashed out. "Meh, you caught that one a lovely ding behind the ear Lou," cackled a witch in an old bathing suit.

A zombie witch cast the first spell. It flared around an old witch and vanished, leaving a set of false teeth laying on the ground. Wearily, Sam flicked her wand and countered it. The old witch reappeared, and punched the zombie in the throat with a fist like a bag of spanners. "Come on then," she yelled, creaking from one foot to the other and holding both fists up. "Who wants some, eh?"

Another zombie lurched forward. The old witch grabbed the new enemy by the front of her dress and head-butted her. The zombie witch fell backwards.

"That's it Enid, stick the head on them, then put the boot in and pinch their wallet. That's the way we done it in the old days."

Blanche Nightly, who normally looked about as dangerous as a damp flannel, stood tall in the middle of a grappling sea of pointy hats. She threw her head back and her eyes rolled crazily in her head. Strange words babbled from her lips. Between the trees, Sam saw a flicker of white. It turned into a wave. Ghosts came flooding through the forest, crashed over the zombie witches, and began to work their poltergeist mischief. Handfuls of dirt were thrown, hair pulled, boot-laces tied together and hats tugged down over eyes.

At Sam's side, Helza was digging in her pockets. As magic began to whizz and simmer above the brawling mass, she shouted "Yes!" held up a small bottle of black liquid, and leapt into the battle with a flying kick that brought a zombie witch to the ground. Sitting on its chest, Helza let a drop of the black liquid fall into the zombie's gaping mouth and then stood, her fist already moving towards another.

Behind her, the zombie-witch clutched at her head, eyes almost popping out. Where the zombie had been, a witch stood up. With clenched fists and a red face, she looked around. "What a flippin' *nerve*!" she yelled, before casting an enormous Force spell that flattened twenty zombies. "Diabolica Nightshade, I'll be wanting a word with you!"

"One!" shouted Helza. "No make that *two*."

THE WHITE WAND

Another witch stood up with a cry of "Of all the blinkin' *cheek*."

Sam staggered forward, her tired legs almost giving way beneath her. A zombie loomed over Helza, who was crouched and dripping potion into yet another mouth. Just as its hands stretched toward her throat, the zombie thing

screeched and lurched off, clutching its rear end and trailing smoke where Sam's fireball caught it.

"Thanks bud," Helza called over her shoulder.

"Ringo," shouted Sam. "Help me." At once, the beetle on her shoulder began calling up magic. The spell the little beetle was working felt familiar. Sam knew exactly what to do. With the last of her magical energy, she cast a Summoning that burst like a silent bomb and rushed out through the trees.

The witches stopped fighting for a second, shocked by the force of the spell. The silence was quickly filled by a low hum. Millions of beetles poured out of the forest and attacked the zombie witches.

Shrieks of pain filled the clearing as beetles small and large crawled into ears and mouths and clothes and began nipping with sharp pincers. Zombies flapped their useless hands and stumbled in circles as black clouds of beetles dived at their faces like handfuls of sharp, chittering gravel.

Sam sank to her knees. She had no magic left and there was another zombie shambling toward her.

"Your broom!" shouted Helza. "Get out of here Sam."

Sam thought about it for half a second – and

pushed the idea away. There was no way she could leave now. As the zombie thing lurched closer, she remembered that Esmelia had once shown her another way of using her wand. With a grunt of effort, Sam threw herself upwards and jammed it up the zombie's nose. Diabolica's soldier screeched and staggered back, tugging at the wand as a fresh wave of ghosts and beetles attacked.

With a sudden grin, Sam called back to her friend, "No way. Not when we're *winning.*"

Unbelievably, Sam was right. The little band of aged witches, helped by ghosts and beetles and ex-zombies, was beating Diabolica's army back. Sam felt a surge of pride for the elderly fighters – the first army in history to go into battle moaning about rheumatism, bad backs and bladder control problems.

So far, Diabolica had stood quietly, watching the battle with a smirk. Now, she held The Black Wand of Ohh Please Don't Turn Me Into Aaaarghh… Ribbett above her head. A bolt of black light screamed into the sky. Around her, the scrum of fighting witches and zombie things fell back. A voice, made magically loud, laughed, "Well, this has been *jolly* good fun, but play time is *over.*"

"*Esmelia*!" screamed Sam. "The White Wand of… Oi You Could Have Someone's Eye Out With That. Use it! For goodness sake, USE IT!"

In answer, a jet of clear white light shot into the sky and began to spiral crazily. "Waaaaaahhh!" screeched Esmelia Sniff.

Diabolica cast a spell. Deep purple lights spilled through the clearing and swept the cloud of beetles away. There was another purple explosion and the ghosts vanished.

The Black Wand of Ohh Please Don't Turn Me Into Aaaarghh… Ribbett flared again, tossing witches and zombies aside, and making a clear path between Diabolica and Esmelia. The old witch was holding onto her hat with one hand, yelping and fighting with The White Wand of… Oi You Could Have Someone's Eye Out With That. Magic sprayed everywhere, turning witches and zombies alike into a selection of white doves, rabbits, and strings of handkerchiefs.

Diabolica stepped forward, laughing. "Oh badness me," she called. "It's Esmelia Sniff, the Most Superior High and Wicked Witch. Lawks, I'm in for it now."

With another giggle, Diabolica flourished The Black Wand of Ohh Please Don't Turn Me Into

Aaaarghh… Ribbett. A slim stream of perfectly aimed magic knocked the wand from Esmelia's hand.

"Ouch," yelled the old witch, sucking her fingers. "Right, that's *it*. Now I'm gonna mess you *right* up."

Diabolica looked Esmelia up and down, taking in the stained vest, disgusting bloomers, nobbly knees, and filthy false beard. Throwing her head back, she laughed a cruel laugh, as only a power-crazed evil sorceresses can. Around her, The Battle of Sawyer Bottom screeched to an end with a few scattered moans and screams and shrill complaints. Without the help of beetles and ghosts, the small army of old witches was hopelessly outnumbered. Diabolica's shuffling things pressed in on every side.

On her hands and knees Sam watched as The White Wand of… Oi You Could Have Someone's Eye Out With That dropped into the mud in front of her. With a scowl she reached out and picked it up.

26 Curse of the Mummy

Diabolica stepped through the mud until she was face to face with Esmelia. The Black Wand of Ohh Please Don't Turn Me Into Aaaarghh… Ribbett whipped out and caught the old witch under the chin.

"Mess *me* up?" sneered Diabolica. "Mess me up? I don't think so, you repulsive, foul-smelling crone. If there's any messing up to be done around here, I'll be the one doing it." She pressed her wand harder into the skin beneath Esmelia's chin. "Do you know what?" Diabolica continued. "I am bored out of my head with frogs. *You*, I think, can spend the rest of your short and miserable life as … let's see… An *earwig*. Yes an earwig will suit you perfectly. And I say 'short' and 'miserable' because after I've turned you into an earwig I am going to jump up and down on you singing 'Ding Dong the Annoying Old Bag Is Dead' until there's nothing left but a splatter of icky goo."

"Oh blah, blah, blah de blah," spat Esmelia. "Never stops talkin' does you? You keeps on goin' yabber yabber yabber…" Like a stinging bee, Esmelia's finger shot out and poked Diabolica in the eye. "…Until someone pokes you in the eye."

"Owwww, curses, you filthy old bag," screeched Diabolica covering her eye with a hand and staggering back. "You'll suffer for that." The tip of the Black Wand of Ohh Please Don't Turn Me Into Aaaarghh… Ribbett began to glow. Diabolica pointed it at Esmelia's heart.

Esmelia blew on the tip of her finger. "Perfect results, every time," she cackled.

"Stop!"

Every head in the clearing turned. Sam was on her feet, her legs trembling beneath her, and dripping with so much mud she looked like a badly chewed chocolate bunny. But beneath the brim of her battered hat flashed green eyes that burned with anger and, in her hand, the White Wand sparkled. "Don't you dare touch her, Diabolica Nightshade," Sam said quietly.

Diabolica blinked her good eye in surprise. "But she just betrayed you and stole your wand, darling. Or did I *miss* something?"

"Just step away and drop The Black Wand of Ohh Please Don't Turn Me Into Aaaarghh… Ribbett," hissed Sam. "And *please* stop calling me 'darling'."

Diabolica smiled. "Why would I do that, darling?" she said with a warm laugh. "I am, after all, your *mother*."

A gasp ran around those witches in the clearing who weren't zombified and there was much blinking with surprise.

"Did you hear that Enid? She said she was the little one's brother."

"Funny old world ain't it? You'd never guess they was brothers to look at them."

Blinking with surprise seemed to be catching and, now, it was Sam's turn to catch the dreaded blinking disease. She blinked, then scowled, "You're not my mother. You're crazy as a bag of hens."

Diabolica walked the few steps to Sam, and smiled down at her, whispering, "Silly girl, you know it's true. Look into my eyes." She stopped and shot a one-eyed glare at Esmelia who was gaping along with everyone else. "Well, look into my *eye*."

Sam looked into Diabolica's good eye and, at last, knew the truth. Just as she had done, deep down, for months. Even while the blood drained from her face, Sam realised that she wasn't surprised. Bubblingly angry: yes. Terrified: certainly. Horribly horribly disappointed: without a doubt. But not surprised. In a flash, the young witch understood that the reason she had badgered and prodded Lilith about her mother so often was because she so desperately wanted to be told it wasn't true. Without ever admitting it to herself, she had longed for her grandmother to tell her that *anyone* other than Diabolica was her mother. Even Esmelia would have been an improvement…

Sam glanced at the old witch gaping behind Diabolica, and decided that actually it would be a neck and neck race between the two in the "Worst Ever Mother" competition.

A tear spilled down her cheek. "Oh Lilith," she groaned. "How *could* you?"

"What?" said Diabolica. "What on *earth* has Lilith Dwale got to do with anything?"

Sam stared miserably into her mother's face. The lonely tear on her cheek was joined by a few friends. "You don't know?" she asked. For a second, she wondered if she ought to protect Lilith's secret, but the cloud of misery inside her flashed the lightning of rage. What had Lilith done for her, except keep the horrible truth hidden? "Lilith Dwale is my grandmother," Sam breathed. "Which makes her…"

"*My* mother. Badness me, tricksy old Lilith," laughed Diabolica. "Well, we're quite the witchy family aren't we?" She reached out and laid her hand on Sam's shoulder. Her daughter flinched and shrugged it off. Diabolica looked down at her a little more coldly. "Anyway, now we've had this *lovely* reunion you'll be coming back to the Bleak Fortress with me, of course. And, if you're a very *very* good little girl, one day you might get to rule the world at mummy's side. Won't that be nice?"

"D'uh, no *actually*. Sam won't going anywhere with a total fruitloop like you." Helza stepped forward and put her arm around her friend.

"Igor," smiled Diabolica. "I should have known *you'd* come crawling out from under a rock. And still not learned any manners, I see. But not to worry, I'll crush you along with these old folk."

"No," interrupted Sam. She knew what she had to do. The old witches had to be saved at whatever cost and she was too tired to protect them. They might be the only hope of stopping Diabolica from taking over the world. "If you agree not to harm anyone in this clearing, I'll come with you. But if you touch a single hair on their chins, I'll fight you. The Black Wand of Ohh Please Don't Turn Me Into Aaaarghh… Ribbett against The White Wand of… Oi You Could Have Someone's Eye Out With That. You against me. Until only one of us is left."

Diabolica tapped her lips with The Black Wand of Ohh Please Don't Turn Me Into Aaaarghh... Ribbett while she thought about it. Her eye swept over the gaggle of old witches, and settled back to her shivering, mud spattered daughter. "Well," she said eventually. "You don't look in much of a state to fight darling, but... well, alright. Just this once, as a little present from me to you, I'll let the old folk live. Most of them probably won't make it to the end of the week anyway."

"I wouldn't count on it. They're tougher than they look," said Sam.

"Except Esmelia, of course," continued Diabolica. "That vile old baggage poked me in the eye and what kind of power-crazed evil sorceress would I be if I didn't be-earwigginate her?"

"No," said Sam firmly. "You'll leave Esmelia alone too."

"Why do you care after she took your wand?"

Sam glanced at the scowling Esmelia. "That's just Esmelia being Esmelia," she sighed. "She may be a nasty, traitorous, wicked old witch, but... well... she's sort of... kind of... in some ways... almost... well, a *friend*."

Esmelia's eyelids flickered. Someone with a microscope might have seen her blinking back a very

very small tear. "Bah," she spat with a shaking voice. "You ain't takin' the little maggot anyways. She's my apprentice she is. Only the Most Superior High and Wicked Witch can cut the bonds between a witch and her apprentice and *officially* that's me. It said so in *The Cackler*, it did. So she stays with me 'till I says so. That's the law that is."

"*You*, Most Superior High and Wicked Witch?" answered Diabolica between chokes of laughter that stopped, suddenly, as if she'd flicked a switch. "But there's an easy way to sort this out. The law also says that she stops being your apprentice if you die." She flicked The Black Wand of Ohh Please Don't Turn Me Into Aaaarghh… Ribbett toward the old witch.

Sam was faster. Without thinking about it, she flung magic towards Esmelia. It was the spell she remembered best because it was the first one she had ever cast. A spell that made an object disappear from one place and appear in another. This time though, she was much, much quicker. And with The White Wand of… Oi You Could Have Someone's Eye Out With That she didn't need to bother with the words and tricky gestures. White light streamed from The White Wand of… Oi You Could Have Someone's Eye Out With That. It burned around Esmelia for a brief moment, giving her just enough time to say, "Aa…" And then she was gone.

The spell took the last shred of Sam's energy. With tears still rolling down her cheeks, her knees buckled. She closed her eyes and collapsed.

Diabolica bent down and plucked The White Wand of… Oi You Could Have Someone's Eye Out With That from her unconscious daughter's hand. "That was *very* naughty of you young lady," she hissed. "Consider yourself *grounded*."

She straightened up and her gaze swept over the clearing. "OK, well done all you shuffling mindless things. But we have what we came

for, so someone pick the girl up and let's get back to the Bleak Fortress. It's *terribly* chilly out here.

"Kill. Now. Di-a-bol-i-ca?" mumbled a zombie, shaking a captive witch.

Diabolica glanced down at the two wands in her hand and at her daughter. "Hmmm…" she said. "Good question. But no, leave them. We've got the girl and the wand. They're no danger to us now."

She turned to go, then turned back and pointed at Helza. "But bring that one. All those dungeons and not a single prisoner; it's such a waste of good torture equipment."

A small group of very very old witches watched as a swarm of broomsticks disappeared into the night.

"Well, Enid," said one. "I don't know about you, but I didn't like *her* much at all."

"No, you're right Dot. She was a right pranny weren't she? I seen her type before of course. If you don't nip them in the bud they gets up to all sorts of nonsense. What *she* needs is a good kick up the rear."

"It's war then, is it, Enid?"

"I should think so Dot. War of the witches, eh? And at our age too."

"Well, you know what they say about old witches, don't you?"

"What, that we smell like something what's gone rotten down the toilet?"

"Well, yes. That. Of course, *that*. But also that we're vicious old beggars what it don't do to get on the wrong side of if you wants your face to stay the same shape."

"Oh yes Enid, that too."

Epilogue

Sam's eyes blinked open in panic and her mind whirled: *Esmelia. Helza. Where were they?*

She sat up and looked around. Beneath her, soft white pillows gambolled like spring lambs, and a white duvet nestled against her like a friendly cloud. A merry fire crackled in the grate opposite and, on the floor, thick carpet looked as though it would swallow her feet up to the ankles. Outside a tall, arched window, snowy mountains were just begging for rosy-cheeked children to race down them on toboggans.

"Do you like it? I've done some redecorating. All that stone was so 500 years ago, And the freezing drafts? Brrrr."

Sam slumped back on the pillows, noting that her hair was soft and shiny. It felt like someone had washed it in silk. She glanced down. Even her fingernails were clean, which was an all-time first.

She glared at Diabolica, who was leaning against the mantelpiece, twirling The White Wand of… Oi You Could Have Someone's Eye Out With That between her fingers.

"I wonder why it's white," Diabolica said. "Black is the *traditional* colour for black wands, after all."

"It's because *I* made it, and I'm a *good* witch," Sam said quietly.

"Is that *really* what you think?" Diabolica said. She seemed surprised. "And I suppose, deep down, you believe the Esmelia Sniff baggage is a really nice person too, do you? The sort of dear old lady who's kind to children and loves kittens."

"At least *she* doesn't want to make everyone into a mindless drooling zombie *thing*," Sam snapped.

Diabolica ignored her and swished the wand backwards and forwards in the air. It left a trail of glittering white sparkles behind it. "It's quite amazing though. Really, I'm very proud of you. I'm not sure I could have done it myself." She stopped and stared at Sam. "Tell me, what does it feel like when you hold it? Is it wonderful? Like you have so much power you could do anything? Change the world and make it whatever you wished?"

Sam blushed. Then nodded slowly.

"Aaah," whispered Diabolica. "So you *are* my daughter."

"…Aaaargh," screeched Esmelia Sniff. For a moment she clawed at nothing, and then dropped like a witch who has just appeared out of thin air into thin air. "Aaaaaargh," she screamed again as thin air rushed past her. "Aaaarrrrgh, blinkin' aaaaargh."

There was an enormous splash. As is always the case when someone falls into a pond or lake, Esmelia sat up with water squirting from her mouth like she was a not-very-ornamental fountain. There was a lily pad on her hat, and a frog.

Esmelia sat in the lake for a few moments, cursing Diabolica Nightshade, then blinked as a torch shone into her eyes.

"Good grief, Esnojeffreybumser is that you?" boomed a deep voice.

"Ummm… errr.. oooo… aaah… yes. Yes it is," squealed Esmelia, in her best dog-strangled voice.

"What happened to you? You're in a terrible state man," gasped Professor Sebastian Dentrifice. "My word, your beard's fallen out and, if you don't mind my saying, those are… well, *ladies* undergarments you're wearing.

Was it some kind of... *torture?*"

"Oh drat," muttered Esmelia. She stood up, dripping water and tadpoles and yelled, "Alright, if you must know. I ain't a wizard, I'm a *witch*."

There was a pause.

That went on for a bit.

In the dark, Professor Sebastian Dentrifice pulled at his beard and blushed furiously. Finally, he squeaked, "Are you *sure?*"

"Course, I'm sure," snapped Esmelia. "Look. I got warts and creepy-crawlies in me hair and hardly any teeth and I'm a skinny old crone with a face like a dried up old bogie."

Professor Dentrifice looked. "Phwwwoooooarrr," he gurgled. "Hubba hubba hot lips. Toot toot! Foxy laaaaydee! *Phwwwoooooarrr*!"

Esmelia sat down with a sigh and a splash. *Wizards*! she sighed to herself. They were all the same. Then she remembered how she came to be sitting in a muddy lake in her underwear in the middle of winter. "Right then," she muttered. "It's like that is it? War! A fight.

Me against Diabolica? Good against Evil?

The frog jumped from Esmelia's hat to her knee and looked into her face accusingly. For a second, its eyes glowed.

"Oh alright then," snapped Esmelia at Cakula von Drakula, "Not-Very-Good against Evil."

Dripping pond water and muttering to herself, Esmelia splashed her way to shore. As she brushed past the gibbering wizard she dipped a hand in his pocket and gently lifted out his wallet. After all, it didn't do to let standards drop. Then, she began squelching her way towards the Goblin's Elbow, where a hot bath didn't await her.

In the moonlight, Esmelia stopped, held up her finger and stared at it. She may have lost her clothes and been shocked to find out that the maggoty apprentice was Diabolica's daughter and dropped into a stinky pond, but she *had* poked Diabolica in the eye, so the day hadn't been *completely* wasted. Anyone looking closely might have noticed a twitch at the corner of Esmelia's lips that might, just, possibly have been the beginnings of a smile. If there was one thing Esmelia Sniff loved, it was a fight.